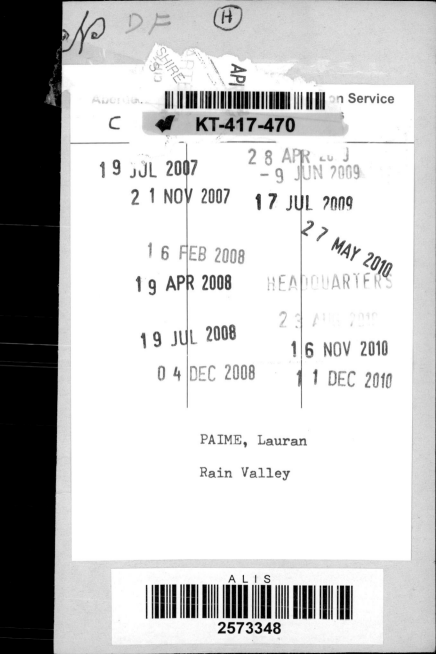

PAIME, Lauran

Rain Valley

Other *Leisure* books by Lauran Paine:

RAIN VALLEY

LAURAN PAINE

LEISURE BOOKS NEW YORK CITY

A LEISURE BOOK®

February 2007

Published by special arrangement with Golden West Literary Agency.

Dorchester Publishing Co., Inc.
200 Madison Avenue
New York, NY 10016

ISBN 0-8439-5783-2

The name "Leisure Books" and the stylized "L" with design are trademarks of Dorchester Publishing Co., Inc.

Printed in the United States of America.

Visit us on the web at www.dorchesterpub.com.

RAIN VALLEY

TABLE OF CONTENTS

RENEGADE RIFLES

CHAPTER ONE

Captain Daniel Fury. Appropriately named. Lieutenant Russell stomped angrily across the parade ground and little wisps of dust arose from the slam of his booted heels.

The Army at its best was bad enough, and Apaches on the warpath didn't make life any easier, but now this new captain from back East, with his regulation bearing, clean uniform, and orthodox manner, was almost unbearable.

Lee Russell passed an enlisted trooper and ignored the man's salute. The soldier looked surprised and shrugged; even the good ones had their bad moments. Lieutenant Russell was known as a soldier's soldier. A little lax, perhaps, but a good officer and a real man. The soldier shrugged again and ambled off toward the mess hall.

Russell entered his log hutment and slammed the heavy pine door with more force than was necessary. Thirty-eight miles since morning with his troop under a blistering sun, and now this replace-

ment officer had ordered him back out with his men
for nightly scouting duty. Damned fool. He'd learn
about this frontier; he'd learn to sweat until his soul
writhed in misery, and his thoughts would turn to
stealing water from the enlisted men. He'd learn
about hostiles, too; he'd see men without eyeballs in
their sockets and without tongues and scalps. Russell's normally good-natured, strong face was un-
pleasant in its anger. He smiled grimly, harsh lines
etched acidly around his large mouth. Damned fool.
Russell would make it a point to break this dandi-
fied pig if it was the last thing he ever did.

Under strict order from Captain Fury, Lieutenant
Russell's B troop moved off on fresh horses after retreat and mess. No one said much; even the troopers
who stood retreat were outraged at this order that
made dog-tired men ride out twice in the same day,
when the fort was full of men who hadn't been in a
saddle for thirty-six hours.

B troop was grim-faced, and a smoldering fire lay
deeply in the pool of red-rimmed eyes as the cavalrymen left the fort behind. Sergeant Ludwig rode
just behind Lieutenant Russell. When the fort was
far behind, he began to swear in a throaty monotone
with a heavy Teutonic accent. The lieutenant listened for several moments before telling him to shut
up. He enjoyed hearing his subordinate swear, because the non-com was doing exactly what he himself wanted to do; Russell knew, as did every man
who could hear the sergeant, who Ludwig was
swearing at.

B troop rode north by west. They were to follow
the Overland Trail for the customary fifteen miles,
make a large circle, then return to garrison. The
same routine every time. By now every hostile for

500 miles knew that cavalry patrols out of Fort Walker always made the same circle.

Russell rode at the head of the silent, glum troopers, and weary thoughts chased one another through his tired mind in time to the muffled *clop, clop* of his horse's hoofs. The first year on the frontier had been like this. Patrols every few days, interspersed with occasional guard detachments for wagon trains of settlers and freighters going farther West. Then the Apaches banded together and began to wage war in earnest. They were fighters unequaled in history—ruthless, more deadly than sin, awesome fanatics. Russell shook his head. Why the United States was willing to have good soldiers slaughtered, just to keep this burned-out corner of hell, was beyond him.

The hostiles were lethal and treacherous when they were sober, but now it was *tizwin* time, when they gathered far back in the bleak mountains and held their annual drunk.

The moon was eerily opaque, the desert lighted by white, watery opalescence. B troop came up on the trail. They bisected it, and followed deeply ground-out ruts for mile after mile. The troopers talked in undertones among themselves in order to stay awake. It was difficult to fight off the desire to doze, especially when the horses rocked so gently and rhythmically along in the cool night.

Routine patrol. Lieutenant Russell turned and beckoned Sergeant Ludwig forward. The non-com kneed his mount until he was riding stirrup with his superior. "Sergeant, did you ever think how nice it must be, not to be a soldier?"

The broad-faced sergeant nodded slowly. "*Ja*, often haf I tought a solcher I vouldn't be if ofer again I had id to do."

Lieutenant Russell smiled to himself in the shadows. Otto Ludwig wasn't as big as Germans are supposed to be, nor did he have blond hair or blue eyes. He was powerfully muscled and flat-faced, with the broad hips and slightly bowed legs of a peasant. "Well, why in hell do you sign on again each time your stint is up?"

Ludwig smiled and shrugged a little apologetically. "Vell, Lieutenant, each dime I go avay from de bost I feel lost." He frowned and scratched his leathery neck. "Vy is dis, I don't know, only dot it is, so each dime I sign on again."

Russell nodded.

B troop had almost reached the turn-off where they would begin their great circle that would take them back to garrison and bed, when somewhere ahead, borne on the clear night air, came a rifle shot.

Russell held up a gauntleted hand and the suddenly alert troops came to a smart halt. The night was quiet except for a distant coyote giving tongue to the moon. An owl, large and swift, swooped knee-high along the desert floor in search of food. B troop sat quietly, straining every ear. Lee Russell was about to ignore the shot as the recklessness of a *tizwin*-happy hostile when two more came faintly to his ears. He raised his arm in order to advance, when a fusillade of gunfire broke out. With a slashing movement in the air, the lieutenant's arm rose and fell and he jumped his horse out into a gallop. B troop, wide-awake now, thundered along behind him.

The sagebrush rocked by in the moonlight, and startled night animals scurried wildly out of the way of the slim blue column of bronzed cavalrymen. Gunfire was intermittent now, as though a siege was in progress, and the noise grew steadily louder.

In front of B troop was a gentle land swell, the type of rolling land that is so prevalent in Southwestern deserts, as though left behind by long vanished oceans in their march toward the sea. Lee Russell slowed his horse to a walk and, without orders, his troops followed suit. Slowly, cautiously the officer breasted the land swell and studied the moonlit desert ahead. At first he didn't see them; then, eyes accustomed to the shape of familiar things, he noticed three large objects in the near distance that were not natural to the earth. He squinted hard and made out the shapes of three shadowy Conestoga wagons, their great, gray, canvas tops slack against the bowed saplings beneath, looking for all the world like skeletons of prehistoric monsters with rough, gaunt ribs beneath starved hides.

As Russell watched, stabs of orange flame leaped from the brush on both sides of the wagons, and answering daggers of lurid flame snarled back from the wagons. Russell turned to Sergeant Ludwig who was sitting his horse calmly beside him.

"Sergeant, ride down the column and tell the men that we'll ride out on the desert east of the wagons. Tell 'em not to make any more noise than they can help . . . and, Sergeant, dispatch two of the men to the fort with a report of where we are and what we're doing."

Sergeant Ludwig rode slowly down the column, giving the orders, while Lee Russell sat his horse with gloved fists resting on the swells, watching the eerie battle. This was very unusual. Indians, in general, did not fight at night; in fact, they would go out of their way to avoid a fight after sundown, because of a prevalent belief that warriors killed at night would never find their way to the hereafter and would have to spend eternity in the dark world of in-between.

Sergeant Ludwig rode up beside Russell. "De men know vot ve do." He squinted shrewdly at the dark outlines ahead.

The lieutenant nodded and half turned in his saddle. The blue line behind him was motionless; even the horses appeared to understand the need for quiet. Russell nodded again toward Ludwig and rode at a walk out toward the eastern desert on his right. Sergeant Ludwig motioned the troops to follow and, wraith-like, with only a minimum of scabbards rattling against saddlery and squeaking leather, B troop followed their officers.

When he could no longer see the Conestogas, Lieutenant Russell halted the troop, aligned it into one long blue line, and ordered an advance. Sabers flashed in the watery night and B troop advanced behind their lieutenant, ghostly and specter-like, their sun-darkened faces blobs of gray, unearthly shadows under the cool, wet moonlight. Sergeant Ludwig smiled wolfishly; the pale light outlined the high spots of his features and darkened the less prominent areas, giving his face an old, evil appearance.

B troop came upon the embattled Conestogas and broke into a reckless charge over the uneven and brush-studded terrain. The marauders, taken completely by surprise, were almost ridden down before they heard the soldiers coming. Too late they saw B troop, and most of them took to their moccasined heels with the fleetness of brush rabbits, ducking and dodging among the rank undergrowth. Some, more angered than prudent, stood upright and traded shots with the troopers. Here and there avenging sabers slashed and cut in the pale light as the 'soldiers paused to give individual battle to the hostiles.

If the country had been devoid of heavy brush, the battle could have been prosecuted with tactical precision. As it was, each soldier was a clean target for the crouching braves—mounted, they were chest-high above the vegetation. The Apaches, on the other hand, could and did take every advantage of the darkened and shadowy brush to fight from concealment.

As Russell rounded a particularly heavy growth of greasewood, a lithe shadow detached itself from the ground and streaked through the air to fasten itself around the officer's neck and shoulders with a grip of constricting rawhide. Russell was dragged from his shying mount and landed heavily with the Apache on top of him. The smell of sour sweat, horsehair, and animal fat struck the lieutenant's nostrils even as he looked up into the wild eyes of the hostile. Locking his legs desperately around the man's middle, he strained mightily and lunged for the throat.

The brave was young and corded all over with supple, hard muscles. He twisted away from Russell's lunging hand and his heavy knife darted through the air. Russell saw the knife coming and half rolled, so that it missed his throat and slammed into the earth. Grabbing at the knife arm, the officer held on for dear life, and exerted every bit of strength in his powerful legs around the hostile's mid-section. The man grunted and his shadowy face quivered under the powerful pressure. His eyes glazed, and Russell could feel the strength in his arms waning. Giving an extra, desperate squeeze that made the muscles of his neck stand out like small ropes, the cavalryman strained with every bit of power in his body. The brave shook violently, his head rolled forward and the strong-smelling body went limp. Russell forced himself to arise, but his legs were wobbly and his lungs felt as if they were on fire.

As the officer rose shakily to his feet, Sergeant Ludwig loped up, took in the situation at a glance, and, without a word, he leaned far forward in his McClellen and thrust his saber through the limp body.

In the gloomy light of late night, B troop rode among the brush pockets, searching out the attackers. Rifle fire had lessened—pistol fire intermittent and scattered. As the skirmish came to a ragged, slow halt, Lee Russell found his horse, mounted, and rode up to the three wagons.

He had forgotten his tiredness during the excitement of the battle. Now, sitting his horse beside the tall Conestogas, reaction set in and the officer felt completely exhausted. With a strong effort he held himself erect as the immigrants crawled out of the prairie schooners.

"We're sure obliged to you, Lieutenant. Iffen you hadn't come along, I've a notion we'd 'a' been done fer."

Lee Russell looked solemnly at the tall, lean teamster who spoke. The man was hard-looking and dirty, with a heavy auburn beard that covered almost all of his face. Evidently the beard was his pride and joy because, while his trousers and shapeless jacket were marred with ingrained dirt and axle grease, his beard showed evidence of much care and combing. The officer felt an inner dislike for the sinewy freighter.

"Where are you bound?"

The teamster grinned ingratiatingly and showed white, even teeth through the background of thick beard. "We 'uns is jist a-travelin'." He shrugged and leaned on his Hawkins rifle. "Immigrants, you might say."

Russell looked over the four or five men, and even in his tired state it dawned on him that there were no women or children among the immigrants. A suspicion grew in his mind. "Well, if you're just traveling, you surely have a destination in mind, haven't you?"

Again the tall man shrugged, but, before he could open his mouth to reply, a shorter, compactly built man with small, slate gray eyes and a slash for a mouth muscled through the group and faced the mounted cavalryman.

"We're bound fer Walnut Creek an' the tradin' post there, although I don't see as it's ary o' yore affair."

Russell turned his head slightly and looked down at the truculent speaker. "Mister, *anything* on the frontier is the Army's affair, if the Army chooses to make it so."

The officer and the teamster exchanged long stares and open dislike was plain on both faces.

The man with the auburn beard laughed uneasily. "Ain't no call to get sore." He smiled at Russell. "You'll have to excuse Lem, Lieutenant, he's a mite upset over them hostiles a-jumpin' us."

Russell regrouped his troop, examined the injured, of which there were seven—but none seriously hurt—and aligned them on each side of the wagons on the return trip to Fort Walker. The lieutenant was frankly puzzled by several things. In the first place, the wagon men hadn't been overly grateful for the Army's interference in their battle; in the second place, if they were immigrants, as they claimed, it was the first time he had seen immigrants without their families. And why were they so evasive about their destination?

The lieutenant was turning these things over in his mind when Sergeant Ludwig rode up beside him. He turned to his striker. "Sergeant, you've been out here eight years . . . did you ever run across immigrants caravaning without their families before?"

The sergeant shook his head slowly. "Dese men is nod immigrants, Lieutenant."

Russell raised his eyebrows. "I don't think so myself, Sergeant, but what makes you so sure?"

Ludwig grunted. "Lieutenant, dem vagons vas moofing ven attacked dey vas. De dracks vas plain behind de vagons, but dey ended right vere attacked dey vas . . . vhich means dot dey don't iffen haf durned around or got off der trail do make der camp." The sergeant shook his head negatively. "Dem immigrants vas traveling at night, vhich means dey aind't immigrants at all, but maybe freighters, an' den de vomen und kids dey don't haf mit."

CHAPTER TWO

The sun was just breaking over the horizon when B troop wound its way back into Fort Walker. The immigrants were left outside the fort by orders of the commanding officer, who allowed no civilian wagons on the military reservation. Lee Russell dismissed his troop, and he noticed, with a twinge of resentment against the new captain who had ordered him out the night before, that his men's faces were drawn and gray with dark, shallow patches beneath their eyes. When B troop had fallen out, Russell turned his weary mount over to Sergeant Ludwig, and headed for the log house that was combination home and office for the commanding officer, Colonel Goodan.

Colonel Goodan had an enviable Civil War record but now he was old—too old; he stayed on at Fort Walker because of a military system that kept men on active duty long past their physical ability to perform the duties of their positions. He smiled, nodded at Lieutenant Russell, and motioned the weary officer to a chair. Russell accepted, despite the frown of Captain Fury, clean and freshly shaven, standing beside Colonel Goodan's desk. *Protocol and regulations be damned*, Russell thought, *I've earned the right to sit*.

"Well, Lieutenant, what happened?"

Russell ignored the captain and faced the colonel.

"We were on the Overland Trail, about fourteen miles from the fort near our turn-off, when we heard firing. We investigated and found three immigrant wagons under attack. We relieved 'em, routed the hostiles, an' escorted 'em here. They are camped outside the fort now."

Captain Fury, conscious of Russell's animosity, was smiling smugly, but his eyes held an intent, interested gleam. "Why didn't you send back a courier?"

Lieutenant Russell arose and faced the captain. "I did, sir . . . in fact, I sent back two."

Fury's smile was edged with dislike. "I was on duty, Lieutenant, and no troopers from B troop reported in."

Russell's anger was softened by surprise. "Are you sure?"

The captain's face reddened and his smile faded. "Are you suggesting that I wasn't on my post, Lieutenant?"

Lee Russell's eyes flamed and anger coursed through his veins. "Listen, Captain, if you don't like me, we can settle that between ourselves at our own convenience, but you'd better learn that out here on the frontier we have to operate as a team or we're going to get wiped out. I am *not* insinuating that you were not on post, at all . . . but I *am* interested in what became of my two couriers."

Fury's face was livid and he took two steps toward Russell. Colonel Goodan, surprised and angered, pushed himself to his feet. "Gentlemen, gentlemen! Remember where you are!"

The two officers straightened into attention at their superior's words, but their eyes remained locked in challenge.

The colonel pushed his shoulders back with visible effort and his watery blue eyes glared at the junior officers. "Gentlemen, we have a deadly foe to vanquish and we'll not do it by fighting among ourselves." He faced Captain Fury. "Daniel, are you certain that couriers from B troop did not report in at the fort?" The captain nodded stiffly. Colonel Goodan sat down stiffly. "Then, Lieutenant, I am confident that your men never reached the fort . . . possibly they were ambushed." The colonel's eyes assumed their weary look. "Go get some rest, Lieutenant, you've certainly earned it." Russell saluted and left the room, rancor heavy in his chest.

B troop turned to in full complement for retreat and mess. They were freshly shaven, bathed, and fed, and, except for slow-burning resentment, they appeared none the worse for their sixteen hours in the saddle and their skirmish with the night raiders.

Sergeant Ludwig and Lieutenant Russell sat in the latter's hutment and played checkers. It wasn't orthodox, but, on the frontier, Army discipline was pretty much left to the discretion of the officers themselves, as each troop had to operate as a team. Lee Russell was known to be lax in this respect.

"Dose vagons left aboud noon."

Russell looked up from the checkerboard; he had

forgotten about the teamsters. "Dammit. I meant to go out an' have another talk with those men."

The sergeant nodded slowly. "Somding vas funny alridt. Corporal Monahan vas on der gat ven dey bulled oudt, und he said dey vas all at vonce in a hurry."

Lee Russell made a move that cost him two black ovals that Sergeant Ludwig took greedily.

"We should have searched those wagons."

The sergeant shrugged. "Vot could ve haf found?"

Russell made a move, baiting a trap for the sergeant. "Damned if I know . . . but maybe we could have gotten an idea about the men, or some lead on why they traveled at night." Ludwig ignored Russell's trap, feinted with a red oval, drew Russell into a trap of his own, and jumped a man. Lieutenant Russell frowned. "Damn you, Otto, here I am trying to figure out the mystery of those freighters an' you're robbing me blind."

The sergeant laughed shortly. "Vot stumps me is vot to our couriers happened."

Russell's eyes clouded. "Well, like Colonel Goodan said, they were probably ambushed on their way to the fort."

Ludwig nodded. "Ja, I dink zo mineself . . . but dot means hostiles vas behind us as vell as in der front, too. I didn't see no sign of dot. If dey vas trailing us, den dey had goot reason, und maybe dey knew vot was in de vagons und vanted it pretty bad."

Lieutenant Russell was about to answer when an urgent bugle blast cut into the still night. Both men jumped to their feet and dashed outside.

Lieutenant Russell loped across the parade ground, toward a little knot of men on the porch of Colonel Goodan's command post. When Lee came up, the colonel turned to face him, and his face looked very old in the flat, white light. "Lieutenant, this man here"—jutting a gnarled thumb in the direction of a buckskin-clad frontiersman—"rode over from Walnut Creek, and he says the hostiles are attacking the settlement and the ranches over there."

Russell turned to the stranger. The man's face was covered by a two-days' growth of beard and his eyes were squinted from long habit. At his belt hung a heavy Kiowa-Apache scalping knife in a beaded sheath, with a tiny scalp lock of coarse black hair suspended from the bottom of it. A shiny Colt Navy pistol was shoved into his broad, mahogany-colored belt, and the fringed shirt and trousers were offset by bead-encrusted moccasins.

"How did you come here?"

"I was comin' to the settlement from the mountains to get rid of some furs, an' I first seen a band of bronco Apaches trottin' through the hills toward Walnut Creek an' they was armed to the teeth. I hid out an' watched fer a spell, an' directly I seen fires springin' up at the outlyin' ranches. Then I heard gunfire, an', after a bit, I seen what looked like the whole damned settlement bust out in flames. By then the firin' was almost deafenin', even as far away as I was. I figgered I'd do better by comin' over to the fort than by gettin' into the scrap, so I cached my furs an' rode like hell fer Fort Walker." The man shrugged his head. "Iffen you fellers don't get to horse, they ain't goin' to be nothin' much left by the time you get over there."

Colonel Goodan put a hand on Captain Fury's sleeve. "Captain, take A and F troops and relieve the Walnut Creek settlement at once."

Fury saluted smartly and ordered the bugler to sound the call to arms.

For the second time in two days, Fort Walker was the scene of furious nightly preparations for the field. A and F troops were to horse in less time than it takes to tell about it, the excitement of their destination spreading like wildfire throughout the fort. With a bellow from Captain Fury, they thundered out of the fort, and, with another bellow, swung southeastward and were swallowed up by the night.

Lieutenant Russell watched Fury's detachment go out the massive gates with mixed emotions. He had wanted to be along the first time the new captain went into combat. He was still staring after the troops when Colonel Goodan walked up beside him.

The old man was more stooped than usual and his face was somber. "Lieutenant, sometimes I wonder if a man can ever stop fighting."

Russell felt a twinge of pity for the tired old soldier beside him, and he glimpsed himself, reflected in the colonel, after twenty or thirty years in the service. "I don't think so, Colonel. Men will always fight. They may talk and dream of peace and plan for it, but inside they all know peace is an illusion and there never will be peace."

Colonel Goodan looked up in surprise. "You're quite a philosopher, Lieutenant."

Russell shook his head. "No sir, not a philosopher . . . just a realist."

The colonel smiled wanly. "Well, Lee, I've known that what you just said is the truth for over fifty years, but until tonight I've never admitted it . . . even to myself." He clasped his hands behind his back and looked out over the still night landscape. "It doesn't make a pretty picture, does it?"

The lieutenant shook his head. "No, sir, it doesn't."

Colonel Goodan scratched his cheek and shrugged.

"Well, Lee, to get back to the present situation . . . you'll take your own B troop as well as D troop and start after Fury at sunup."

Russell faced his commander. "That'll only leave C troop at the fort, sir."

Colonel Goodan smiled. "But don't forget the three Gatling guns, Lieutenant . . . they're worth a troop in firepower."

Lee Russell nodded and saluted. The colonel returned the salute and watched the lieutenant walk off, satisfaction and approval in his sunken eyes.

Sergeant Ludwig was waiting when Russell returned. He had heard the news of the attack on Walnut Creek. The two men stood and talked for several minutes under the overhanging eaves of the officer's quarters.

"You might as well pass the word along, Sergeant, that B and D troops will turn out at reveille to take the field. We're to follow Fury's force as reserve and mop-up troops."

The sergeant nodded as he yawned. "Vell, at least ve don't in der middle of der night go again, anyvay."

Russell grinned at the insinuation. "No, but if Fury had had his way, I'll bet you we'd be on our way to the settlement right now, instead of A and F troops."

Ludwig frowned slightly. "Vot's wrong mit dot captain anyvay?"

Russell shrugged. "Search me, Sergeant, but since the first day he came onto the reservation, he's had it in for me, for some reason." The lieutenant smiled sourly. "Of course, I haven't done anything to make him like me, either."

The sergeant pulled his gauntlets out of his belt

and thoughtfully pushed his broad hands into them.
"Vell, vhen de officers each udder don't like, id's
sure hard on de men."

Russell laughed and slapped Ludwig roughly on
the shoulder. "See you at sunup, Sergeant, ready to
ride."

Before the light of a new day broke over the fort,
troopers were busy getting their gear ready. Reveille
found few men of either B or D troops asleep. As
soon as mess was over, the men were lined up, in-
spected, given formal orders, and marched off.

Riding at a slow lope, B and D troops hunched
forward in their saddles to offset as much as possible the cold of an early autumn morning. Lieutenant
Russell rode in the lead, as usual, with Sergeant
Ludwig directly behind him. The only stranger with
the troops was the frontiersman who had stayed the
night at Fort Walker, having no stomach for night
fighting, and who now rode stirrup with Lieutenant
Russell.

The lieutenant was curious about his new companion and studied the man out of the corner of his
eye. "Are you a trapper?"

The man rubbed a calloused hand along his un-
shaven jaw. "Not exactly. I'm a kind of explorer. I
trap when the trappin' is good, an' just poke around
the back country when it ain't."

Russell digested this thoughtfully. "Do you know
where the hostiles hold their *tizwin* drunks?"

The man nodded curtly. "Sure. Lots of mountain
men know them spots. In fact, most of us has been
on a bender or two with the Injuns."

Russell faced the man as their mounts loped

along in the clear, roseate, early morning light. "Would you scout an Army detachment to them?"

The man in buckskin looked across at the officer in sharp amazement. "You'd get massacred unless you was to outnumber 'em ten to one."

Russell shrugged. "We could do that, too, if we knew how many there would be."

The frontiersman shook his head. "Nope, on secon' thought I don't allow I'd do it. Couldn't no good come of it, an' a helluva lot of bad would sure crop up. Nope, I ain't yore man fer that job."

Russell dropped his conversation with the mountain man. It was an idea of his that, if the Army could catch the hostiles at one of their *tizwin* drunks, it could break the back of Apache resistance once and for all. He was wrong, but, since he never had the opportunity to put his scheme into operation, he never knew it.

Walnut Creek was a small settlement along an all-year creek of good fresh water, where a number of rich ranches had sprung up. The settlement itself was no more than a large, log trading post, with a blacksmithing shop attached, a rough slab-sided saloon called The Bounty, six or eight log buildings that housed either employees of the trading post, or other tradesmen of the village—such as horse traders, trappers, and livestock dealers, as well as freighters with their mounds of axles, wheels, replacement parts for their great wagons, and the wagons themselves.

Lieutenant Russell heard the noise of battle while his troop was still quite a way from the settlement. He stood in his stirrups and looked ahead. There was a billowing cloud of smoke, black and oily, rising over Walnut Creek. The closer the cavalrymen got to their destination, the louder the roar of battle became. Apparently fighting had been in progress all night, and was still raging with all the fury that marked Indian warfare.

There was no quarter given or asked. Generally speaking, an Indian war was fought with the stubborn, unreasoning deadliness that knew no truce, no armistice, and no peace until one side—often both—was so decimated and exhausted that it could no longer fight.

Coming into sight of the burning village, Russell was horrified to see that all of the buildings—with the lone exception of the trading post—were burning furiously. Apparently those settlers who had been able had made it into the trading post and were making their stand there.

Confusion and dense smoke swirled with every change of a vagrant breeze and marked what once had been a beautiful, picturesque little hamlet in the partly cleared meadow land of Walnut Creek.

Lee Russell deployed his men and charged into what remained of Walnut Creek settlement. The cavalrymen unsheathed their sabers and hurriedly, nervously tucked the flaps of their revolvers under their belts behind the butts of their heavy pistols. With a scream that was equal in wildness and ferocity to anything the hostiles could offer, Russell and his veterans swept down into the mêlée, with the outraged and vengeful wrath of old campaigners coming to grips once more with their sworn and hated enemies.

CHAPTER THREE

Captain Fury's troopers were firing from a hundred vantage points, their faces drawn and smoke-streaked. The arrival of Russell's troops helped morale, but the fight was not over by a long sight.

Afoot, their horses abandoned to whatever fate lay in wait, B and D troops ran for cover, leaping over the bodies of Apaches, settlers—men and women, and occasionally a child.

The hostiles were in force—much greater force than the Army had reason to expect. Russell studied the hiding places of the braves and was surprised to see that not only were Chiricahuas among the enemy, but also Mescaleros and Tres Piños. Too, there were hostiles that he couldn't place at all, their dress being altogether foreign to Apache apparel. Suddenly the grim and amazing facts unfolded to him, and he turned to Sergeant Ludwig.

"Sergeant, this is some kind of a hostile confederacy. We've got a real battle on our hands."

The sergeant, carbine in hand and kneeling be-

hind an upturned freight wagon, squinted at the
wraith-like Indians slipping among the ruins and
the brush out on the meadow.

"I noticed somding doo, vhen running for cofer I
vas." He pointed at the stiff form of an Apache
killed the night before. "De rifles de hostiles has got
is already der latest repeating block guns. Dose
guns is brand new, Lieutenant, brand new."

Lee Russell stared at the fallen brave's rifle and a
sick feeling hit him in the pit of the stomach. Someone was bringing the latest repeating rifles to the Indians. It had to be a white man; an Indian couldn't
buy one. His eyes moved slowly over the crumpled
forms of the dead and stopped on the upturned face
of a tiny girl with baby-blue eyes, a piquant freckled
little nose, and a rosebud mouth, her auburn hair a
coppery shroud around her.

Russell stared in fascination at the little girl's hair.
It was auburn, the same color as the beard of the
teamster who had been attacked out on the Overland Trail two nights before. Russell knelt beside
Sergeant Ludwig. "Otto, I'll tell you what was in
those wagons we escorted."

The sergeant was shocked by the wild look in his
superior's eyes. "The wagons had rifles in them,
Sergeant, brand new rifles for the Apaches . . . repeating rifles to kill settlers." His arm pointed stiffly
at the little girl. "Quick-firing rifles to do things like
that with."

Ludwig grabbed Russell's arm. His face was
harsh. "Get aholt on yourself, Lieutenant. Iffen you
vas right, ve a fight still haf . . . man, get aholt on
yourself."

Lee Russell, white-faced and shaking, lowered his

eyes. "You're right, Otto. It was that little body in the foreground."

The sergeant nodded and swallowed. "I know," he said with simple dignity, "I saw dot, alzo."

Lieutenant Russell crawled over the hot, seared earth toward a group of troopers firing from behind two dead horses. The ripping slash of a bullet tearing it's way into one of the animals made him drop flat. "Keep your heads down, boys, keep your heads down!"

The troopers glanced at him briefly. "Lieutenant, we got a war on our hands."

Russell risked a look over the bulwark of brown hair. "Yes, an' those devils have repeating rifles . . . so don't take any chances, because they don't have to reload like we do."

The soldiers looked at one another, white-faced, and a corporal Russell recognized as belonging to A troop voiced their thoughts.

"You ain't tellin' us nothin' we haven't known since we pulled onto the field last night, Lieutenant. An' we think they must've gotten them guns from a white man."

Russell nodded. "Unless I'm wrong, Corporal, they got 'em from those three wagons B troop brought in night before last."

The soldiers swore obscenely, and their jaw-muscles rippled beneath their sweat and grime-streaked faces.

Sergeant Ludwig found two dead troopers from A or F troop behind a gutted sheep shed. He looked at the four dog-tired soldiers still alive. "You fellers vith Captain Fury come last night?"

One of the soldiers nodded. His eyes were red and deep in his head. "Yeah, but we ain't seen the captain since we hit the settlement."

A deafening thunder of rifle fire broke out. The sergeant instinctively flattened out on the ground. He could see the dense brush along the creek from between logs that had the chinking knocked out. There were hundreds of half-naked bodies writhing and sneaking among the cover. He poked his Sharps carbine through a hole, aimed at a partially hidden brave whose flat face was snuggled low over the stock of a brand new repeating rifle, and squeezed the trigger. The carbine bucked and roared, its report lost in the deafening thunder of close combat, and the victim jumped straight up out of his hiding place, stood erect for a full two seconds, then crashed, headfirst, into the hard earth. The sergeant smiled to himself as he reloaded.

A and F troops were badly cut up. Slipping and crawling from one cover to the next, a boot heel shot off and two holes in his trousers, Russell searched in vain for Captain Fury. None of the troopers who had ridden with the captain had seen him since the Army had come to the village. The lieutenant assumed that the captain had been killed in the opening engagement, and appointed several non-commissioned officers of A and F companies to take over under him. There was little need for Army regulating, however, and the lieutenant knew it—this was a fight to the death and each man was for himself. But in order to maintain some sort of discipline, should the need arise later, Russell, nevertheless, made the appointments.

* * *

Two hours later, the fighting was just as ferocious and undecided as it had been all night. The hostiles were fanned out, however, after finding that by concentrating their forces along the creek they were being cut to ribbons by the reinforced soldiers. Now, instead of fighting only a frontal battle, the troopers suddenly found the wary braves slipping around behind them, and picking off exposed troopers from the rear. Blue-clad cavalrymen ran frantically for new cover, something that would protect both front and rear at the same time. Here and there the darting figures would crumple under the accurate and withering fire of the hostiles.

Lee Russell lay behind a small pile of firewood with a broken oaken barrel behind him, leaving only his long legs exposed. Firing methodically and with deadly marksmanship, the lieutenant sought out targets in comparative security. Through squinted eyes, he watched a short, squat man motion to another hostile and point to a cluster of burned-out logs that once had been a small house. The two spoke briefly for a moment, then the summoned hostile slipped away among the brushy growth, evidently to carry out an order.

Russell's face drew into an expression of exultation and blind hatred as he rested his carbine on a flat rock, took deliberate aim, pulled the trigger, and looked up. The Apache, apparently some kind of a leader, was hit in the side near the ribs by the officer's bullet, and the force of the slug knocked him violently backward. He lay thrashing, clutching at his side where a gaping, ragged hole was pouring out blood onto the dry earth.

Lee Russell smiled grimly, and his teeth were

white beneath flattened lips. It was good to kill when there was need. He felt the surging pulsation of hot blood through his body, and his narrowed eyes sought another target.

The dying man was jerking spasmodically when a sweat-streaked young buck darted out of the brush, grasped him by the shoulders, and tugged him to safety among the buckbrush and mesquite. The younger man's eyes were large and somber as he watched the older warrior gasp out his last breath. He rose into a crouching position and began a relentless, stalking advance toward Russell's place of concealment.

The settlers in the trading post were giving a good account of themselves. They had an indisputable advantage over the exposed soldiers. From every shattered window and door, from cunningly whittled loopholes and cracks between the logs where the chinking had been knocked out, rifles bristled.

The hostiles had tried to storm the building twice; both times, they had been repulsed with mounting losses. Dead braves lay under the windows and across the long porch of the building, but none had succeeded in gaining entrance. The Indians had tried to fire the building, but that had failed, too. Giving up direct assault, the deadly children of the desert had retired to places of concealment, where they could fire on the building—but they seldom got a good target. With the coming of Fury's command, the Indians had unleashed all of their pent-up rancor on the soldiers, with devastating results.

Running, sliding, and crawling, Sergeant Ludwig had made what he thought was a fairly complete round of the trooper's posts. He had been shocked and horrified at what remained of Fury's two troops. Dead cavalrymen were everywhere, torn scalps evidence that the hostiles had been counting coup all night long.

Suddenly, from behind an overturned outhouse, the sergeant and a startled Apache ran almost into one another's arms. Both men stood transfixed for a long second in complete surprise, then, like striking snakes, they brought up their guns. In the fleeting fraction of a second before the hostile fired, Sergeant Ludwig recognized the heavy dragoon pistol in the Indian's fist as belonging to a trooper, and he jerked the trigger of his own gun. The Indian's revolver went off, missed the sergeant by a fraction of an inch as the hostile swung abruptly away from Ludwig in a half arc, then collapsed in a heap. For no particular reason, except that he resented seeing a brave with some dead trooper's pistol, Ludwig bent over and picked up the revolver from the hostile's dead hand. The unconscious movement saved his life—as he bent over, the Apache, who had been stalking Russell's hiding place, couldn't resist the temptation, and fired at Ludwig's back. The Indian's bullet smacked into a thick plank on the old outhouse and Sergeant Ludwig dropped flat, trying to squirm around to face his adversary as he fell.

Lieutenant Russell, attention drawn to the little drama by the closeness of the hostile's shot, swung around and in a glance saw the Apache raising his shiny new rifle for another shot at the desperately squirming sergeant. He threw his pistol in a flashing arc and thumbed two rapid shots at the exposed Indian. Neither shot took effect, which the officer hadn't expected anyway, but they did startle the brave enough for his own shot to go wild. The

Apache swung around and tossed his rifle to his shoulder when he saw Russell, but Sergeant Ludwig, taking careful and deliberate aim, fired once, and the Indian fell forward without sound or movement.

The Indians were leaving. Lieutenant Russell noticed the slackening of the firing from the creek and the brush around the settlement before he actually saw the Indians slinking to their gaudily decorated horses, mounting, and riding off with their shiny repeating rifles. He bellowed like an enraged bull for his troopers to concentrate on the enemy's horses, but the range was too great, and the feasibility of advancing over the cleared land toward the hostile mounts was suicide. So, in helpless fury, the lieutenant had to lie there and watch the hostiles ride away.

By late afternoon the dead had been assembled in one place, identified, and covered with great dirty slabs of canvas taken off the few ruined wagons around the settlement that had escaped burning. The battered defenders came from within the trading post and assembled in dogged and grim silence as civilian casualties were counted and recorded in Lieutenant Russell's little black book.

There were hysterical, choking sobs from women, and gaunt, dry moans from men. The scene was well calculated to bring lumps to the hardest throats among the veteran campaigners and many an eye was feverish as the story was told by Ephraim Callahan, the owner of the trading post.

"We was just finishin' the day's business last evenin' when the devils attacked. They had been hangin' around all day, in larger numbers than usual, an' we was a might uneasy, then in come three Conestogas in charge of some freighters we never seen before. The wagons went directly to the Injun camp down in the willows near the creek, where a lot of noise was goin' on." The storekeeper shook his head slowly, as though to erase a bitter memory before he continued.

"Them Injuns was still on their *tizwin* an' were awful noisy. We could see the teamsters doin' a lot of tradin' an' arguin' with them, then, all of a sudden, the Injuns jumped into the wagons an' began passin' out brand-new repeatin' rifles. I told my hired man to round up the folks in the settlement an' come into the store, for I figgered we was in fer trouble. Two of them renegade freighters come a-runnin' up here, after they fought clear of the Injuns, and I let 'em in . . . I wanted 'em as prisoners." The man shook his graying head again, and his tired, red-rimmed eyes looked unseeingly into Lieutenant Russell's face.

"You know the rest of it, Lieutenant. A couple of troops of cavalry hit the settlement about ten o'clock last night, an' their captain rode right up to the store an' took the two teamsters out. That's the last we seen of 'em."

A woman, with a lock of jet-black hair hanging forlornly from beneath her bonnet, stepped up. "No it ain't, Ephraim. I seen them two men grab horses an' mount up, then they rode off in a dead run with that soldier feller with 'em." The woman wagged a finger under Russell's nose. "An' they went West, young man, away from the settlement an' away from the direction of Fort Walker!"

Lieutenant Russell was nonplussed. After his cursory search for Captain Fury, he had assumed the man had been killed and had looked no further.

Now the implication behind the woman's words and actions regarding the senior officer left him but one conclusion to draw. Captain Fury, somehow, had been tied in with the teamsters who had brought the guns to the hostiles. "Did one of the freighters have a thick auburn beard?"

The woman nodded vehemently. "Yep, one had a red beard an' the other one was dark, like a Mexican or a 'breed." She nodded again. "An' they both rode off with that officer." Lee Russell questioned several other settlers, and each told the same story. Having been in the trading post, most of them had seen the entire episode.

CHAPTER FOUR

It was a gloomy, grim procession of cavalrymen who wound their way back toward Fort Walker. The ragged remnants of A and F troops led a large band of saddled, riderless horses, while B and D troops carried vast loads of gear taken from fallen comrades. There wasn't a word said, and the setting sun, red and swollen, shone dully on the line of grimy, tattered, and exhausted troopers.

Lee Russell, numb with exhaustion and grief, rode slumped forward in his saddle, his thoughts black and shot through with despair.

Sergeant Ludwig looked at his superior with somber eyes with a glint of steel in their outraged depths. "Ve should go after him."

Russell nodded mechanically.

"Id's der first time effer I heard of such a ding." The sergeant was a long time getting over the initial shock of finding out that Captain Fury was a renegade. "In der Army such dings don't happen."

When the badly mauled blue column rode

through silent guard on the gate at Fort Walker, an orderly called Colonel Goodan. In horror, the commanding officer watched the troops line up. He walked out to Lieutenant Russell as the junior dismissed the men. "What happened, Lieutenant? Good Lord, man, the troops are only half here."

Russell looked into the commander's eyes. "There aren't any more coming, Colonel. That's all that's left."

"Was it an ambush?"

"No, sir. It was a battle against a hostile confederacy of some kind, and the Indians were armed with brand new repeating rifles." Russell's pent-up emotions broke through the floodgates of his military reserve, and, in a torrent of profanity, he told the colonel the story of Captain Fury's treachery.

In the command post, Colonel Goodan sat slumped over his littered table, vacant-eyed and very small. Russell felt acute pity, but there was nothing he could do or say. "This is the end for me, Lieutenant." Goodan shook his head as though to clear his thinking processes. "After a lifetime in the service, disaster has found me out here on the frontier."

Russell raised his eyes from the floor. "Colonel, let me take my striker and a squad of men. I'll bring him back."

The colonel nodded abstractly. "Yes, Lieutenant . . . yes, indeed. Go after him. Bring him back here, dead or alive, but bring him back. At least we can salvage the regiment's honor by executing him ourselves."

When Russell left Colonel Goodan's office, the old man was still sitting at his desk, nodding his head gently in the gloom of early evening, his eyes staring straight ahead but seeing nothing—unless it was the ghostly specters of his long years as a soldier, marching down the corridor of time until they halted in the disgrace of what had happened at Walnut Creek.

Lee Russell passed the word to Sergeant Ludwig, who in turn picked out four men he knew as old campaigners and staunch career soldiers, and who had also been at Walnut Creek. They made up their packs, silently, looked to their arms, then turned in and got a full night's sleep because, as Ludwig bluntly told them, no one knew when they would get to sleep again—unless it was "nefer to avaken."

At dawn, under the approving stares of their regiment, Lee Russell, Otto Ludwig, and four lean troopers trotted stiffly out the gates of Fort Walker. They were back in the shambles of Walnut Creek by early morning.

Asking questions everywhere he thought might be uncovered what he could use, Russell and his squad canvassed the stunned settlement thoroughly. The only man who had shrewdly thought out the captain's position was the same buckskin-clad mountain man who had ridden to Walnut Creek with B and D troops the day before. Russell noticed three new drying hanks of hair tied to his knife-sheath as he talked to the man.

"I figger the hostiles was too drunk to hold to their bargain of buyin' the guns, Lieutenant, an' jist naturally jumped this here captain's freighters, took the guns, then run amuck."

Lee nodded impatiently. He had all this figured out for himself. "But where could they go?" He couldn't bring himself to refer to Fury by his Army title.

The buckskin-clad man shrugged. "A hundred places, providin' they didn't lose their scalps whilst they was goin' there. In fac', iffen I was in this here captain's boots, I'd head south into Mexico. It's a cinch he don't dare go near any whites, an' the Injuns'll kill him out of hand, because he ain't no use to them no longer."

Lieutenant Russell thought over Fury's plight and was inclined to agree with the deductions of the mountain man. He summoned Sergeant Ludwig, rounded up his squad of enlisted men, and they left Walnut Creek on the Overland Trail, heading southwest into the new day.

The day was far spent when a vedette Lieutenant Russell had posted to ride a mile or so ahead came loping back. He reported a large band of foreign hostiles crossing the trail several miles ahead.

Russell nodded. "After what happened to them yesterday, they probably are going to wherever they came from."

Sergeant Ludwig smiled sourly. "Dey haf had enough. Dey lost a lod of men und didn't get nodding much for it bud a few scalps."

The vedette frowned and spoke in the drawl of Texas: "An' them new repeatin' rifles."

The little squad of soldiers rode off the trail and wound through the brush until they found a good spot protected by dense growth where they sat on their horses and watched the Indian band on the move. The bearing of the soldiers was straight-backed and bitter. In their silence they drew only small satisfaction from the obviously dejected attitude of the decimated Indian band.

Nightfall found the troopers near enough Fort North to see the pale yellow lights shining over and through the barricade walls. They kept in the saddle, and an hour or so later, after mess and retreat, arrived at the gate. After an introduction and an explanation of their errand, the troopers from Fort Walker were billeted for the night.

At Fort North a regularly employed Indian scout, by the name of Samuel Custer, volunteered to join the hunt for the renegade Captain Fury. Lieutenant Russell agreed after the scout pointed out that he alone, among them, knew the short cuts and the Indian camps south to the border.

At sunup the troopers were astride and, with their new companion and guide, rode south on the trail until the sun was directly overhead. At the noon bivouac, near a busy little creek, the cavalrymen made a meal while the scout turned his horse and descended the hill until he was out of sight, dismounted, and crept back toward the crest where, lying prone, he watched two slow-moving horsemen. They were Mescalero Apaches.

Custer jumped on his horse and rode back to camp. He told Russell of the oncoming Indians, and the soldiers hastily hid in the willows along the creekbank until the Apaches were almost directly in front of them, then they rode out, pistols pointed navel-high. The Apaches froze, realizing that flight was synonymous with death.

In camp, one of the Apaches proved to be a communicative fellow called Blue Bear. He was a Mescalero who had come west to join the Chiricahuas in a raid against a white settlement, where the hostiles were to be sold the latest repeating rifles. He told the white men that the *tizwin* drunk had made all of the Apaches eager to fight, and, when an Army officer told their leaders at Painted Rock that he would sell them rifles, the word spread. Soon the entire Apache nation, and several neighboring tribes, joined exultingly in the transaction.

Lieutenant Russell, through the scout, Custer, asked Blue Bear if he knew where the white Army officer was. The Apache nodded. He had seen him in the company of two other white men riding south on the Overland Trail only that morning, many miles ahead.

That settled it. Russell didn't want to send a man back to Fort North with the Indians, so he was forced to release them—which he did over the savage and growling protests of the scout, who wanted to execute them, then and there. Russell read similar sentiments on the faces of his troopers and managed to save the Indians only by ordering an immediate breakup of camp.

The Apaches rode away from the bivouac without a backward glance, but they kept right on loping their horses just in case the whites changed their minds. The soldiers rode hard behind the scout, who suddenly turned off the trail and struck a narrow, dusty game trail through a narrow cañon. "It'll cut miles off the reg'lar trail."

At sundown, the cavalrymen and their fringed companion were in a maze of brush-covered hills. The scout assured them that by noon on the following day they would be ahead of their prey. They ate a dry supper because they were in a hostile country and didn't dare make a fire. They didn't sleep, either, but they could and did rest their horses. The night hour went by slowly for the lounging men. Talk was held to a minimum as an added precaution, although the scout told them he doubted if there were any hostiles in the immediate neighborhood—their dry camp was far south of the general route of travel the Apaches used between United States territory and Mexico.

While the stars were still high in the heavens, the little party saddled up and rode slowly behind the scout, who picked his way carefully down the narrow trail. This was poor country to lame or cripple a horse in; many danger-studded miles lay between a white man and help.

When the daylight hours had crept over the cold land, the searching party was again on a well-defined roadway that led into Mexico. After several hours of hard riding and studying the tracks over which they rode, the scout called a halt near a clump of stunted pines. The men unsaddled and hobbled their horses. They were weary and cold and the sun felt good on their tired bodies.

Lieutenant Russell squatted in the shade under a ragged old pine near the scout. "Are you pretty sure they haven't gone by us?"

The scout was industriously pushing tobacco out of a beaded pouch into an old pipe. "Yep. The only way they could 'a' got ahead o' us was if they rode all night, an' I didn't see no fresh sign on the trail that'd tell us they did." He popped the pipe into his mouth and sucked on it, unlit. He smiled at the lieutenant's puzzled look. "I seldom light it on the trail . . . smoke's too strong. Injuns might smell it, an', as well as I like to smoke, I like my hair better."

When the sun was straight overhead, Russell sent a scouting trooper afoot up to a low hill that commanded a back view of the trail. The man came back almost instantly and reported four horsemen coming at a trot down the trail. One, he said, was an Indian. The other three were white.

Custer grunted and picked up his repeating rifle. "That'll be our men. Probably got an Injun confederate along to guide 'em." He shrugged eloquently and casually. "So much the better."

Lieutenant Russell passed the word that he wanted Fury alive, and both the teamsters, too, if possible. The troopers faded into the shadows of the brush and trees. The scout and Sergeant Ludwig took up position partly in hiding, rifles in the crooks of their arms, deceptively relaxed-looking.

When the riders hove into view, Russell recognized Fury and the teamster with the auburn beard. The other man was the short, belligerent freighter who had told him to mind his own business the first night he had seen them. The officer smiled grimly and his hand hovered talon-like over his pistol butt. When the riders saw the lone soldier in the middle of the trail, they stopped and stared, then urged their horses forward at a slow walk.

Lieutenant Russell looked hard at the ex-captain, who had sloughed off his uniform and had donned fringed buckskins. "Fury, I've been waiting for you."

Daniel Fury, whatever else he was, was no coward. "How did you get here?"

Russell shrugged. "What difference does it make? I'm here, and I'm going to take you back to Fort Walker, either astride or feet first."

Fury laughed in a short, nasty way and turned to his companions. "Shall I kill him with my pistol or my knife?"

The bearded teamster had none of Fury's confidence; he was plain scared and showed it. With a slow, deliberate movement, he raised his pistol toward Russell.

A low-pitched voice broke in on the tense scene.

The scout, Custer, had his carbine aimed at the teamster. "Drop it renegade, or I'll shoot your yellow carcass in two."

The mounted men jerked around in surprise and saw the rifle barrels protruding from the brush on their right. The Apache chose that moment to make a break for it, but, before his horse had gotten into its stride, he was plucked off its back by winged fingers of lead, and lay still on the desert floor.

Fury sat like a statue.

Russell grinned wolfishly. "You didn't think I was alone, did you?"

The renegade's face lost its tense look. "No, I reckon I shouldn't have, but tell me . . . just how in hell did you get here so fast?"

Russell pointed to the lounging scout. "Mister Custer, there, knows every short cut in this godforsaken country."

Fury glanced contemptuously at his dead guide. "An' that liar said *he* knew the fastest way to get here." He cleared his throat and spat. "We even had a day's start on you. All right, Lieutenant, you've got us, let's go back an' get it over with."

Russell looked wide-eyed at his prisoner. "Why did you do it?"

The renegade grunted disgustedly. "For gold . . . what other reason would a man have? I met these freighters in Santa Fé. They told me how easy it would be, an' how much the hostiles would pay in Mexican gold for the repeating rifles." He shrugged his shoulders. "But the damned fools forgot about it bein' *tizwin* time an' that they'd be too drunk to trust. We not only lost our rifles an' our chances of stayin' concealed, but I expect we'll lose our lives as well."

Russell had a picture in his mind of a little girl with a tiny, piquant freckled nose lying stiff in death, a bullet in her chest. "Didn't you think of the settlers?"

The renegade Army officer's eyes flashed blisteringly. "Sure I thought of 'em. You damned fool . . . if it wasn't for them, the hostiles wouldn't need our guns."

The cold-bloodedness of the man swept over Russell in a flash of understanding. Before he thought, he swung his arm through the air with vicious force, and Fury's head snapped backward.

The renegade held his hand over his torn mouth and glared balefully at Russell.

"Fury, I've never liked commanding an execution squad, but I'm living for the day I'll command yours. It's renegades like you, who sell out your birthright and your country, that are adding children's scalps to Indian coup sticks. There's nothing lower on earth than a renegade . . . even an Apache wouldn't stoop to the things you've done."

Few words passed between the soldiers and their prisoners as they returned to Fort North. The scout, Custer, left them there, and they continued on alone to Fort Walker, where they reported in with their captives, exactly four days to the hour from the time they left.

Daniel Fury was first court-martialed and drummed out of the Army, then he was tried as a civilian, subject to military law, along with his two henchmen, and finally sentenced to death for treason, and executed, all in the same day.

With a pale face but a determined set to his jaw, Lieutenant Russell saw the renegades tied to three pine saplings, listened to Fury's taunts, ordered the firing squad.

"Ready . . . aim . . . fire!"

The body of Daniel Fury, fairly weighted down with the murderous lead of the enraged soldiers, sagged limply against the ropes that held him to his execution pillar.

TROUBLE WEATHER

The day was still and wilted. Heat—drought-like heat, the kind that sucked moisture out of the skin of men and the hides of animals—sweltered the town of Colt, Nevada. There was a foreboding stillness over everything. Down the road a hostler was sprinkling hardpan in front of the livery barn to settle the dust, and up where Carter Alvarado stood in the doorway of his saddle shop, looking out, the air was as still as ashes.

Behind Alvarado, in his shop, there was a depth of coolness flavored with the richness of leather smell. It was a good scent, and with it went great skill and craftsmanship. A good saddle maker was more than an artist; he was also a man who could foresee, who could envision things; a man who could work wonders with his hands and work the disconnected facets of a problem into a logical solution. He was both an artist and, in a sense, a seer.

Carter's lean face was bronzed, his eyes clear blue. There was very little surplus weight on his stringy frame, and his smile was both warm and inviting. He smiled when Ned Prouty, the town marshal, went past, perspiring, red-faced, and edgy.

" 'Morning, Ned."

" 'Morning, Carter. Damned heat'll be the death of all of us yet," Prouty said, slowing to a halt. He was a short, massive man, as broad as an oak and nearly as hard. Prouty had always suffered from the heat. Like all fleshy people, it soured his stomach and put an edge to his temper.

"Did you ever notice," Carter said amiably, "how hot days seem to have an odd feeling to them, Ned? Like an explosive stillness."

"I don't even like to think when it's this hot," the marshal said, "but I'll tell you one thing . . . if it don't rain damned soon, there's going to be more trouble bust loose than you can shake a stick at. This drought . . . it's fightin' weather. Makes the range bulls fight . . . makes town dogs fight . . . and it makes men fight. 'Specially the men who've got cattle. They got to stand around and watch the grass burn up, the water holes go dry, and their hay crops shrivel. When folks get pushed up against it, Carter, they just naturally get on edge. You mark me . . . there'll be trouble if we don't get rain."

"That's what I mean," the saddle maker said. "The air gets hot and still. There's something explosive in the atmosphere . . . like invisible dynamite, Marshal. It feels as though the world might explode at any minute."

Marshal Prouty's screwed-up, small eyes lingered on Alvarado's face until the sound of a loping horse behind him drew his attention away. "Who'd be riding a horse like that in this weather?" he said irritably.

Carter looked east along the vacant thorough-fare. "It's that colonel from the Indian reservation," he said.

Neither of them moved as the colonel, seeing Prouty, veered over, dismounted almost before his horse had halted, and stepped up under the over-hang with a short nod at the marshal. He was a whipcord man with an upturning mustache that like his hair—and his eyes—was gray. He wore an air of authority as though born with it, and, when he looked at someone, they had the impression he could, and would, compel them to do some dis-agreeable task. Ned Prouty set his big legs wide and returned the colonel's nod with one just as brusque.

" 'Morning, Colonel," Prouty said, "sort of hot to be ridin' like that, ain't it?"

The soldier brushed the question aside with a glance. "Needs must when the devil drives," he said.

"Uhn-huh," Prouty said, not comprehending. "Well, if it's drunk soldiers you want, I ain't got any."

"I wish that was it, Marshal."

"A deserter?"

"Indians, Marshal. Indians. The beef drive is late."

"How late?"

"Ten days."

"Well," Prouty said, "that's happened before."

"Not this time of the year it hasn't. They started drifting in from the back country about two weeks ago, Marshal. Pitching tents around the agency . . . hundreds of them with their infernal dogs, horse herds, and children. They've been sitting around out there for two weeks waiting . . . waiting. The grass was gone last week. This week it's their pemmican and jerky that's run out. They've been eating horses and dogs, but those are thin. Now they're getting restless. They've started gathering . . . holding councils . . . and the eternal malcontents are at it again. . . ."

"Stirring up feuds?" Carter asked.

"Yes. The entire tribe is uneasy. It's been so infernally dry this summer and fall." The colonel looked at them. "Do you know what will happen next?"

Both Prouty and Carter nodded at him. "They'll start holding the forbidden dances . . . the scalp and raiding meetings," Prouty said. "We were just talking. I said you could smell trouble in the air when it's like this, Colonel."

"Have you talked with them?" Carter asked.

"Of course. I told them I'd sent soldiers out to see what's delaying the confounded beef contractor."

"Where's he driving from?"

"Montana. It's that same fellow from Deer Lodge who had the contract last year. Clem Holzhauser . . . damn him. Those cattle were to be at the agency by the First. It's now the Tenth of September and no sign of him."

"The Eleventh," Carter said. "Have you heard from the men you sent out?"

The colonel shot Carter a baleful look. His mouth set in a grim line. "I didn't send any," he said grimly. "I've only got eighty enlisted men. With trouble coming, I don't dare detach a single man." He looked at Ned Prouty. "That's why I rode to Colt today. I want you to go find that damned blundering drover and get those cattle down here as fast as you can."

Prouty looked at the officer with a growing scowl. "I got a town to watch," he said. "Besides, that was foolish . . . to tell 'em you'd sent men when you hadn't."

A dark stain swept upward from the colonel's collar. His granite gaze bore into Prouty. "Would you rather have an Indian uprising?" he asked. "With eighty soldiers I can't afford to let a single man off the post. If those Indians jump the reservation, they'll hit your ranches down here the first thing. Are you aware what that'll mean, Marshal?"

"I know," Prouty said stiffly. "I also know that's just one more damned good reason why I dassn't leave, too." He frowned at the colonel. "Why, for all you know that herd might still be up in Montana."

"No. No, it's quite a bit south of Montana. The last I heard Holzhauser was going south through the Shoshone country."

"Maybe the Snakes jumped him," Prouty said. "Maybe they're short on rations, too."

"I had word from Fort Hall, the Shoshones are well supplied and particularly peaceable this year," the colonel said. "It's nothing like that." He looked from Prouty to Carter Alvarado. "Would you do it? Would you find that infernal drover and make him hurry?"

"What about the Indian Bureau?" Carter asked. "Or some of the Army posts along the way?"

"The Indian Bureau," said the colonel with a great deal of scorn in his voice, "says it's the Army's job. I've asked for men to be sent from Fort Hall, and I've been assured they will be sent . . . as soon as they are available. Now, gentlemen," the colonel said, clipping his words, "why do you think I've come to you? Because I can't get help *anywhere else* . . . that's why!"

Carter's eyes had a vague glint of humor in them. He turned and watched Marshal Prouty. Before Ned could speak, the colonel went as far as his horse and there he looked back. "Do you recall the Wounded Knee Massacre?" he said. "I'd hate to see that happen again, particularly in an area under my control. But I assure you it's not impossible if someone doesn't help me find these damned cattle!"

Carter walked a short distance from the doorway of his shop. "Colonel, if I went . . . and if I found the cattle and got Holzhauser to hasten the drive . . . could you hold the Indians in check until I got back with them?"

The officer answered very frankly. "Probably not. Eighty men don't make a very deep impression upon a thousand Indians, sir, but I promise you and your town . . . and your marshal . . . that everything will be done at the reservation to keep the bucks from going out. I have the confidence of some of the older chieftains. . . ."

"Huh!" Marshal Prouty grunted scornfully. "Those wizened old devils don't have any more influence over the warrior societies than I have . . . or you have."

"You are correct," the colonel said, untying his horse, and bending a long glance full of annoyance upon Ned. "Very correct. But I can do no more."

"Another question," Carter said. "How many cattle would it take to keep the Indians pacified while we find out where the contract herd is and get it to the reservation?"

"Probably three to five hundred head." The colonel mounted his horse. He was ignoring Prouty and looking at Carter with interest. "Time is the important thing, you understand."

"I understand," Carter said, and nodded when the officer whirled his horse and rode up the road. From behind him, in the shade of the wooden awning over the boardwalk, Marshal Prouty made a critical observation aloud and followed it up with a less critical but just as barbed question.

"That nincompoop . . . ridin' down here tellin' me what I got to do to get him out of his own stew . . . who does he think he is anyway?"

Carter returned to his shop, shed his apron, put on his hat, and locked the front door.

Marshal Prouty was continuing on his way down the walk when Carter rode by moments later. At Prouty's questioning glance Alvarado waved a hand, raised a gallop, and left the town behind.

His ride to Will Drago's D-in-a-Box Ranch was through crushing heat, but, when he arrived, left his horse in the shade of rugged old cottonwoods, and went to the spring box for a cold drink, he felt recompensed for the inconvenience even if his mission failed.

Will Drago was old, seamed of face, lean to the point of emaciation, and reputed to be the richest cowman in Nevada. In appearance, though, Drago could have been another of the squatters who were beginning to take up land across Nevada's cattle ranges. He stood in the shade by the spring box, watching Carter drink. While he waited, he twisted up a brown-paper cigarette, lit it, and exhaled. When the saddle maker was hanging the dipper back on its spike, Drago said: "Man'd have to be crazy, in love, or have a scheme, to be out ridin' in this weather, Carter . . . which is it?"

Carter wiped his chin. "That's the best water in Nevada," he said.

Drago fixed him with a knowing glance with the faintest look of humor in it. "Sure glad you like it," he said. "Must be awful dry in town for you to ride 'way out here just for a drink of it."

Carter sank down on the spring box. "I need about four hundred head of cattle, Will."

Smoke curled up around Drago's perpetually squinted eyes. "Well," he said slowly, "I got 'em. I got about ten times that many . . . maybe more, Carter . . . but this sure'd be a helluva poor time to sell 'em. Be hard pressed to render out enough lard for one candle per critter. This drought's just about melted 'em down to hide and horn."

"I can't pay for them, Will."

Drago made a very elaborate study of the distant range writhing under the sun's furnace lash. "You going to give up the shop and start ranching, Carter?"

"No," Carter said, and drew in a big breath of air. "The contract herd's late at the reservation and the Indians are starving."

Drago's expression changed subtly. The squinted eyes drew deeper into the folds of flesh and the craggy jaw locked tight. A forbidding aura settled over the older man, a coldness. Carter sensed it without looking around.

"The colonel at the agency rode to Colt this morning, Will. His drive is ten days overdue, and the Indians are getting restless."

Drago put out the stub of his cigarette, squashed it under his heel, and said: "Don't tell me about Indians. See that lone pine out there with the palings around it?"

"Listen, Will . . ."

"My little boy's buried there. You've heard the story. My only child. Twenty years ago, the Indians come. . . ." The words trailed off and Drago stood looking at the pine tree as though something across the heat-tortured distance was holding his inner attention, and then he relaxed and leaned upon the spring box again. "Carter, if you'd wanted to start ranchin', I'd have let you have the damned cattle. But for redskins . . . no!"

"Listen to me for just a minute, Will."

Drago inclined his head. "Sure, Cart, talk away. Y'know, I always liked you for some damned reason. Maybe because you're an orphan an' in a way so'm I. Sure, son, I'll listen to you anytime . . . you talk and I'll listen." The flinty face turned. "Except when you talk about *Indians!*"

"Will, there isn't another cowman within three days drive of the agency that has his cattle down from the high country. I know how you feel . . . how all the old-timers feel . . . but you surely know what's going to happen if they starve . . . if they go hungry another week . . . if they see their children die. They'll start leaving the reservation. They'll start raids and there'll be killings. . . ."

"I guess folks'd have to protect themselves, then, wouldn't they? You know, Carter, I was figurin' to take the wagon into Colt for groceries in a day or two. Maybe I'd better go today . . . right now . . . and maybe hire me ten, twelve good gun hands. It's been ten years since I killed a damned redskin. Ten years . . . maybe longer."

"You don't mean that, Will."

"Don't I?" Drago was gazing out toward the pine tree again. "Everybody's got hate in 'em, son," he said. "I never hurt no squatter like a lot of the big outfits are doing. I figure Nevada's big enough for everybody. Take those Farrels who started up last spring, about a mile south of me here. Where they squatted has always been my grazin' land, Carter . . . you know that . . . but there's plenty more land . . .

even better than what they fenced off. And y'know, them folks been struggling mighty hard to make a go of it and they're raisin' them two little tykes to be the kind of folks Nevada's goin' to need one of these days."

"I know," Carter said. "I've heard in town how you kept them going through the winter, with a milk cow and beef to eat, and hay. Folks respect you for that."

"I don't need no slap on the back," Drago said. "I do what I figure's right."

"Then think what will happen if . . ."

"But Indians are different. I fought 'em for twenty-five years. I gave 'em a son . . . more'n a thousand head of cattle . . . twice they burned me out."

"You've evened the score, Will. I've heard how you were the best Indian fighter in the territory in the early days. When I was growing up, they used to tell stories about Will Drago and his war with the Indians."

"I never killed enough of 'em, Carter. I never can. I just won't live long enough to kill enough of 'em."

"Think about the folks out here who never had to fight Indians, Will. They wouldn't stand a chance."

"They'll learn mighty fast," Drago said. " 'Specially if a few of us old-timers show them how to hunt Indians . . . how to stalk 'em and ambush 'em."

Carter watched the old man's profile a moment, and then looked away—looked out over the shimmering land.

Drago stirred beside him. "I know you mean well," he said, "but fellers your age come late to maturity, Carter. This is something you younger men don't know anything about. You've never seen a ranch after the redskins left it. You've never had to bury old friends or sit your horse with ten cowboys and watch two hundred warriors drive your herd off." Drago slapped his leg. "Before I'd feed a redskin, I'd starve myself."

Carter said no more. He rode out of the yard with Drago's narrowed eyes on his back. He didn't turn until he came to the fork in the road, then he looked back. Drago was faintly discernible, still leaning against the spring box, an old etching in iron and rawhide. There wasn't an ounce of compromise in him anywhere.

Carter rode south with the white-gold heat flowing outward from a lemon-yellow sun in every direction. After a while he saw the Farrel shack with its lean-to cowshed and boxed-in water well. In the meager shade two small children were playing. They looked up as he approached. One was a little girl about five, the other was a boy, slightly older— perhaps eight—willow-straight, with a shock of sun-bleached hair. The boy watched him a moment, then said: "Want a drink, mister? I'll get it for you." It seemed to be the thing to say and he knew it by rote, but his eyes never left Carter's sleek horse.

"No, but thanks, son. Is your pa at home?"

"No, he went to Colt in the wagon, but my mother's in the house." The boy went closer as Carter swung down. He touched the horse's nose tentatively. "Can I hold him, mister?"

Carter handed him the reins. He went to the door and knocked. A thin, pretty woman appeared in the opening. "My name's Alvarado," Carter said, "I'm from town."

"Come in, Mister Alvarado."

As he entered, the coolness swept over him.

"Would you care for a bowl of milk? We keep it cold in the well box."

"No, thanks. Ma'am, I guess you know the Dragos . . . ?"

"Very well," the woman replied with warmth. "If it hadn't been for Will and Miz' Drago, we'd have starved out last winter."

"I'd like to ask you to do them a favor."

"Well," the squatter's wife said doubtfully, "if there's something we can do for them, we'd most certainly do it, but . . ."

Carter talked. He described how a little boy wore his hair, how he loved horses, how he used to play in the mud around the spring box, and an expression of gradual understanding came into the woman's eyes. When he finished speaking, she looked at the hands in her lap without speaking.

"There are a lot of things old Will's money can't buy," Carter said in finality, "and this is one of them. People are lots of things, ma'am, and most of them are good, but when a man's spent his life fighting, something goes out of him and he can't always find it again, even when he wants to. If he doesn't want to . . . if habit blinds him . . . then someone's got to help him find it. Do you understand?"

"Yes, I understand. Do you think I can do it?"

Carter stood up. His height seemed to tower over her. "Your family likes Nevada, doesn't it?"

"Yes. We've had it hard here, but we like it . . . we're going to stay."

"Then do something for Nevada. Not just for Will, but for Nevada . . . and for yourselves. Pioneers don't come to a wilderness just to *take*, ma'am . . . they come to *give*."

"I'll do it, Mister Alvarado."

He went out to his horse, took the reins, and dug a coin from his pocket that he dropped into the little boy's pocket. "I always pay horse holders," he said, mounting. "The next time your pa brings you to town, come by the saddle shop and I'll show you how saddles are made."

Long after Carter had ridden from the yard, the little boy stood in the dancing heat looking after him.

When Carter got back to Colt and dismounted at the livery barn, a loafer, whittling in the shade, said: "Prouty's been askin' around for you, Cart. Think he's over at the shop now. Leastways, I just saw him cross the road in that direction."

The marshal was sitting on the bench of the saloon next to Alvarado's shop. He got up as Carter approached. "Where you been?" he asked. "Man'd ride in this weather's crazy."

Carter unlocked the shop, and Marshal Prouty followed him inside. It was cool and dingy and the air smelt of leather. Carter tossed his hat onto a cutting table. "Rode out to see Will Drago," he said.

"To get some cattle?"

"Yes."

"Good . . . folks'll owe you a vote of thanks, Cart. When's he going to drive 'em?"

"He isn't."

Ned watched the saddle maker put on his apron.

"He said he wouldn't feed an Indian if he'd starve himself . . . something like that."

Prouty pursed his lips and leaned on the workbench. "All right . . . the damned old fossil. How about the other cowmen? There's bound to be one or two who ain't so butt-headed."

"Name me one, Ned. There isn't a rancher within

a hundred miles who's got his cattle down out of the mountains yet. It'd take a week, maybe two weeks, to find another one who'd agree to loan four hundred head to the agency until Holzhauser's herd gets here."

"I guess so," Prouty said absently. He drummed on the bench and gazed at nothing, then he straightened up. "Got to be *something* done, Cart. If those Injuns jump the reservation, no one'll be safe."

"You can't blame them."

Prouty swore irritably. "Who's blaming 'em? What I'm saying is we got to do something."

Carter looked at the marshal. His expression was saturnine, his voice soft. "Y'can't do much standing around in here, Ned."

But Prouty missed it. His thoughts were miles away. "Must be three, four thousand Injuns at the agency," he said thoughtfully. "If they go out, their cousins at Wind River, Deer Lodge, even the Red Cloud agency'll come down here and join 'em." As an afterthought the marshal said: "I got McMurray to head over toward Fort Hall and see if he could find Holzhauser." Prouty leaned over and began drumming on the bench again. "Cart," he said, "we can force Drago to give us those cattle."

"How?"

"Get a writ . . . an emergency writ . . . make up a posse. . . ."

Carter was shaking his head before the marshal stopped speaking. "You know better than that, Ned. You know how those cowmen have always stuck together. You take a posse of townsmen out there and force Will Drago to loan you the cattle, and he'll call on every cowman in the territory to fight you. A war like that . . . at the same time the Indians are leaving the agency . . . would plunge the whole country into anarchy."

Prouty straightened up off the bench with a flushed, angry face. "All right," he said sharply. "What're we going to do . . . sit around here waiting for the world to explode in our faces?"

Carter looked beyond the marshal, out through the doorway where molten sunlight lay blanched and still. There wasn't a sound, a breath of air; the town was tinder-dry and hushed. "Years back I heard old General Crook say the basis for all our Indian troubles was the almighty dollar. Until today I didn't know how true that was."

Prouty snorted and resumed his drumming on the workbench. "This ain't no time to be worrying about that," he said.

"Do you know why those beef contractors are always late, Ned? Because they spend too much time trying to buy cheap cattle so they can make a bigger profit on their contracts."

"What of it?"

"If that's what happened this time, and there are killings, there isn't a law in the country that you can arrest the contractor under. Not one. The search for the almighty dollar, as Crook called it, might be responsible, but you can't put money in jail, Ned."

"Money's behind it, then," the marshal conceded. "We've still got to get those cattle and drive 'em up to the agency."

Carter went to work fitting a fork covering; the leather was wet and it felt good to the touch. "Come back this afternoon," he said to Ned Prouty. "Maybe one or the other of us will have come up with something by then."

Carter worked for an hour after the marshal left,

then he put his hat on, went across to the livery barn, and talked one of the loafers there into riding out to a little hill on the south side of Paiute Peak—there was a spring there, some shade, and a vantage spot where the watcher could see in all directions. All he had to do was sit up there and drowse—and watch.

On his way back to the saddle shop, Carter stopped at the café on the eastside of the road. There, a handsome woman brought him a glass of lemonade. He drank it neat and asked for another. While he was sipping the second glass, he said: "Missy, did you ever see a scalp?"

"A what . . . a scalp? No!" He drank and she studied his face. "What's the matter, Carter?"

He smiled up at her. "The weather."

Her expression altered to a look of understanding. "I know. It's tense. You can feel it drying out your skin and making your nerves crawl." She looked past Carter to the door and said: "Come on in."

Carter turned around. It was the squatter's wife, Mrs. Farrel. Her face was flushed from the heat and a loose strand of hair hung disconsolately over one small ear. He arose slowly, watching her cross to the bench. When she sank down, he asked for another glass of lemonade.

"Did you do it, ma'am?"

She looked at the glass set before her. "I did it. Yes."

"And . . . ?"

"They left about an hour ago. Will and four riders."

"North?"

Mrs. Farrel cupped her hands around the cool glass when she said: "Yes."

Carter got up. To the girl behind the counter he said: "Could you make up a jug of that lemonade, Missy?"

"Yes."

"At least two gallons of it . . . with sugar in it?" The girl nodded. "And get someone to take it out to the Farrel place?" He dug some silver out of his pocket.

"What's it for, Carter?"

"A little boy . . . and a little girl."

"The Farrel kids? Is this Missus Farrel?"

"Yes. How much, Missy?"

"Nothing. If the bar next door can stand drinks on the house, I guess my café can, too. What's it for . . . a birthday party?"

"No. I've got to go, Missy. If you'll make it and get someone to take it out, I'll tell you the whole story at supper tonight." He touched Mrs. Farrel's shoulder lightly. "Did he say anything, ma'am?"

"No, it was the way he looked. I wished I hadn't told you I'd do it, Mister Alvarado."

Carter squeezed her shoulder and left the café. He was entering the livery barn when someone hailed him. It was Marshal Prouty. "Get your horse," Carter said as the lawman came up. "We've got a little ride to take."

He didn't speak again until they were riding northwest out of Colt. "You know a short cut to the reservation, Ned?"

"Sure . . . why?"

"Ride up there and tell the colonel some cattle are coming. Tell him to send some of his *old* men down to meet them. Remember that, Ned . . . his *old* men. Tell him Will Drago's bringing them."

"Will? You said he refused to do it."

"He did. He turned me down flat. I got that squatter's wife, Missus Farrel, to take her son up to visit the Dragos. Will's a quiet man . . . a thoughtful man."

"What's that got to do with it?"

"He could remember back twenty-five years, Ned. He could remember there was nothing in those days that could save another little tow-headed boy ... nothing. But times have changed. Now, *he* can save a little kid who loves horses. . . . He left with a herd about two hours ago. You explain that to the colonel. You tell him Will's a lifelong Indian hater ... that's why we want him to send his *old* leaders down to get the cattle ... no young bucks with paint on. Now you'd better get going."

"What're you going to do?"

"Meet Will. Go on."

After the marshal left, jogging steadily across the blast-furnace land, Carter Alvarado headed toward Paiute Peak. There he met the man he'd sent out earlier, and together they watched a growing cloud of dust advance down the long, scorched valley. They rode toward it, and by the time Carter could distinguish the cattle, hundreds of them ambling along through the eye-smarting dust, one of five horsemen driving them whirled his horse and rode toward Alvarado. Carter drew up and waited. The rider was Will Drago.

He regarded the saddle maker stoically for a moment, then he said: "Thought a band of bronco bucks was comin' down on you, eh?"

"No," Carter said, waiting for the thoughts in the old man's eyes to be put into words.

"I reckon you didn't, at that," Drago said, never taking his eyes from Alvarado's face. "Y'know, Cart, I'm old, but I ain't simple. That was an underhanded thing you did, boy."

"That's why I'm out here, Will ... to apologize."

Drago looped his reins, made a cigarette, lit it, and exhaled with his head averted, watching the cattle moving past. "Pretty hard to let a kid hold your horse and not expect him to tell other folks he held it, Carter." The slitted, faded eyes swung back. "What other reason would you have to ride by their place?"

"None."

"All right. I'm going to feed your redskins. You made your point. That's all you wanted."

"There isn't anything I can say, Will, except that I'm glad you changed your mind."

"Yeah, there's one more thing you can say . . . that now you're goin' to ride along to be sure me an' my boys don't pot-shoot any of them."

"I'll go back to town."

"Oh, you might as well ride along," Drago said. "No sense in me an' my boys doing all the sweating."

They started out to catch up with the drive. Drago smashed out his cigarette on the saddle horn. "I had a little roan mare, Carter. A boy shouldn't grow up without a horse. Maybe, in a year or two, I could use 'em both, working the cattle."

"You're one in a million, Will."

Drago was looking into the hazy distance. Without taking his eyes from whatever was holding his attention, he said: "If those bucks up yonder got paint and feathers on, you'll find out what I am, boy."

Carter strained to see Indians, but could not. He rode with the herd until it was near the edge of some dusty hills, then, along with the other riders, he finally reined up as a colorful cavalcade of horsemen came out of a shadowy draw.

The tension in the air was heightened when

Drago called to his men and, when they were around him, told them to: "Keep your eyes open and your mouths shut."

Drago sat his horse tall, bronzed and motionless. It was as though a quarter of a century had dropped away; he appeared as tawny, as dangerous as any Indian. In fact, the slit of his eyes, the hawk-like profile, and the leathery color of his skin made him look exactly like an Indian, to Carter.

There were five Indians, all attired in full ceremonial regalia, and, when they were twenty feet away, they reined up, looking at the white men.

Under his breath Will Drago said: "Sioux. Agency interpreters for the damned Paiutes."

One of the Indians raised his arm and rode toward Drago. "*How kola . . . wasicun,*" he said. (Hello . . . white man).

Drago's eyes were squeezed nearly closed. "*How Kola.*"

The old spokesman jutted his chin toward the cattle. "*Waste! Pilamayaya!*" (Good! Thank you!)

Drago relaxed slightly. His expression was mingled reluctance and grudging acknowledgement. He said: "*Sunka tanka zi . . . yuta lela waste!*" A colloquialism meaning "the meat closest at hand is the best to eat," or, literally: "big yellow dog is best eating one."

The old chieftain looked from the herd to Drago's face. "Good," he said in English. "You know old ways, old words. All gone now. Now lies. Now cheat. Now afraid. Now hungry . . . Sioux, Paiute . . . all go hungry. No good." The slitted, black eyes bored into Drago. "You see children go hungry?"

Drago put both hands on the saddle horn and leaned on them. "I've seen children go hungry," he said softly. "Now you round up those cattle and drive them up to your Paiute cousins."

The old man said—"*Nita kola.*"—raised his arm, and signaled for his companions to drive the cattle away. He did not turn and look back, nor did Will Drago take his eyes off the Indians until they were lost in the cloud of dust. Then he turned his horse and without a word started back the way he had come.

Carter rode up beside him. "Will . . . ?"

Without looking around, Drago said: "The Indians used to have a saying, Carter . . . 'Let the deed die with the wind.' You go on back to town."

Carter rode south toward Colt. When he arrived there, slanting afternoon sunlight brought a pall of faint clouds from east of the mountains. There was a coolness to the dusk which hadn't been felt in Nevada for seven months. A coolness that could mean rain.

At the livery barn a man he knew only casually met him. "Howdy, Alvarado," he said. "You seen the marshal?"

"He's up at the agency, but he ought to be back soon."

"He sent me out to hunt up that contract herd."

"Did you find it?"

"Yep . . . liked to kill three horses doin' it, but I found 'em. They're about sixty miles west, comin' slow. The contractor got sore when I told him he was to hurry . . . said in weather like this even walking cattle is too fast a gait."

"I guess he's right," Carter said, and crossed through the cooling air to his shop and sank down into a chair there. He was still sitting when Marshal Prouty came in, his shirt drenched with perspiration.

"God, I hope I never have to live through another day like this one."

"Was that the colonel's idea . . . sending the Sioux, instead of the Paiutes?

"Yep. Was it all right?"

"It was all right."

Prouty looked in surprise at an unopened quart of whiskey on the workbench, beside Carter. "You going to get drunk? I never knew you touched it."

"I don't, but maybe tonight I will, Ned. Wonder if you'd do me a favor?"

"You name it an' I'll do it!"

"I told Missy I'd come back to the café tonight. I won't be able to . . . will you give her my apologies?"

"Sure. What's on your mind?"

Carter got up, put the bottle of whiskey into a coat pocket, and picked up his hat. "I've got to make a call," he said.

"Goin' to make a saddle?"

"No, going to make amends. Going to ride out to the Drago Ranch. See you in the morning, Ned."

RAIN VALLEY

CHAPTER ONE

The first full rays of sunlight struck; the mountains
became a pale, tawny brown, each crag and buttress
sharp-standing in the utter hush. Higher, higher
even than those enormous mountains that dwarfed
a man to nothing, to dust, a sifting of overhanging
sky turned gray, then pink, and finally flashed
golden with a brilliance that made Rain Valley
emerge all at once from the wall of the night so that
the horseman could see where wood smoke rose up,
curving away to hang above the pines and firs, and
where stirrup-high grasses shone with dew in the
clearings and little parks scattered among the dark
thrusts of trees.

The horseman paused when sunlight came against
him, feeling its life-giving substance. He made a cigarette and smoked it, gazing outward over Rain Valley with shoulder muscles loosening and his strong,
sun-darkened face gone thoughtful. His desire was
to sit there, Indian-like, absorbing beauty with a
mind blanked out by this very substantial pleasure,

but instead he urged the horse along until tree shadows hid them both along the serpentine, down-winding trail to the valley floor.

For three days now he had observed no sign of man. A band of elk once, slow-pacing the bony flank of a foothill, and a mother bear with two cubs clawing a bee tree, and, at night, coyotes, heard but unseen, yapping at early stars in a cold, spring sky. For three full days he had bored deeper into these mountains without hurrying, and here, totally unexpected in all this immense vastness of rocks and forests and saw-tooth ridges, was a settled valley.

The sun was high beyond stiff-topped pines, the northern slope fully alight, when shale underfoot gave way to pine needles and tufts of buffalo grass where the trail leveled out into the valley. A boiling creek slashing its way through a tumble of lichened rocks cut crookedly toward a widening ford. Here the horseman crossed, sending trout minnows scurrying frantically at sight of his shadow, and making the only noise in all this stillness when his horse's hoofs sucked up out of the gravel.

Beyond a short distance, the horseman stopped, testing the air. It was clear, thin, and fragrant now with an aroma of coffee and frying meat. He made another cigarette to kill the rising urgency of his hunger and smoked it in calm reflection. Thus far, there was not a living soul who could say he—or she—had seen a strange rider. On the other hand, three days and about eighty miles should provide a wide enough void, and he was hungry, very hungry. His horse, too, was tucked up. He had favored it at every opportunity, but horseflesh went downhill fast in mountainous country. The animal needed a rest badly.

He sat there without movement, shade-dappled by overhead tree limbs, blending into the background, as still and silent as stone. So still a yellow-eyed red-headed woodpecker lit not fifty feet away and made a sharp beat unaware that he was not alone. The horseman watched him briefly. The bird abruptly stopped hammering, cocked its head groundward for only a second, then made a cry and fled. The horseman, too, ran his gaze outward along the creek-bank, caught movement easily, and watched it approach.

It was a girl and that was normal enough, but she was wearing buckskin trousers, and the horseman had never before in his life seen a woman in men's trousers. He watched her go to the creek and bend forward to fill a bucket. The trousers were drawn taut over a firm flank and the woolen shirt swelled with greater-than-average fullness. Then she raised her head and he saw the long, faintly upcurving richness of her mouth with its center fullness. He was seeking her eyes when a man's voice came softly forward, trapped in the silence and shadows.

"Sue?"

The girl whirled, grew erect, and from farther back the horseman saw her gradual stiffening. He looked beyond where a lanky man was coming across matted pine needles without a sound, his hat back and his blanket-coat open to show a deep chest and, lower, a belted gun with an ivory handle, low-slung and functional. The man's face was layered from sun tan; there were prominent cheek bones, and the mouth, parted now in a tentative smile, would normally, the horseman saw, be hard-set and uncompromising.

"What are you doing here?" the girl challenged, resistance in her every line.

"Came by early," the man said, coming on, not halting until they stood no more than three feet apart. "Abel said you'd gone for water, so I figured I'd pack the bucket back for you." He made no move to bend forward where the bucket stood less than a foot away. His dark and bold gaze remained strongly on the girl. "Listen, Sue," he went on, his voice changing, roughening with emotion, softening and roughening. "I'm going up to Brown's Hole t'look at the stock. Why don't you come along? We'd be back by evening."

The girl bent forward, caught up the bucket, and started past. "No, thanks," she said shortly.

"Sue . . ." A strong hand shot out, clamped over her arm, and held fast.

"Take your hand off me, Birch."

His smile died slowly. "Abel's got stock up there, too, y'know. You could sort of see how they're doing. He'd like that, Sue."

"Birch Walton . . . take your hand off me!"

Evidently the man's grip tightened because, back in the shadows, the mounted man saw her lips flatten and her eyes mirror pain. He loosened in the saddle, and then the man was speaking again.

"I think you'll go up there with me, Sue. You can do it easy-like or you can do it hard-like, but you're going."

"I wouldn't go up there with you if you . . ."

"If I what?"

"You're hurting me, Birch."

"If I what?"

The girl gasped now, and from behind the dark man came a faint tinkle of spurs. At first neither of them heeded this, then the dark man let the girl go and whirled. It was too late. A sledging fist caught him with all the force of a felling axe, and he went over backward, his hat spiraling away. He fell silently on the pine-needle matting and did not move.

Without speaking or spending more than one long glance on the girl, the horseman returned to the shadows, got his mount, and returned with it. Then he nodded and reached for the water bucket, and very gravely said: "That food sure smells good, ma'am."

She continued to study him until the moment of total surprise passed, then her violet gaze became alert—not afraid of him, but wary and skeptical. "Who are you, mister? Where did you come from?"

"From over those mountains," he answered with a sideward jerk of the head. "Name's Burt Crownover."

While she considered this, staring directly at him, he saw the lovely column of her neck and the little V where an increased pulse beat stormily. She seemed to balance something in her mind, and she appeared on the verge of speaking when the sprawled man at their feet groaned. She twisted to look down, then she said—"Come on, stranger."—and started through the trees.

Crownover dutifully followed. He was close to smiling.

Just before they emerged into a clearing where a bleached, log house and barn stood, the girl turned. Crownover was still looking amused. She fetched up short, bending a long and hostile look at him.

"Did you think that was funny, back there?" she demanded.

With a face wiped scrupulously clean and set in conventional impassive lines, Crownover made a negative head wag. "No'm."

"That was Birch Walton . . . or haven't you ever heard of him?"

"Never have. But that wasn't what I was smilin' about anyway."

"What then?"

Crownover looked beyond to the log house. He shifted his weight and only gradually returned his attention to the girl. "Nothing. Let's go on, ma'am. I'm hungrier'n a she-wolf."

"Not another step," she flared at him, "until you tell me what was funny."

Crownover looked around at his horse. He thumbed back his hat and ran one palm down the outside seam of his breeches, but he said nothing and it was clear in his face that he did not intend to.

"Mister," the girl said flintily, "you'd better ride on."

"No breakfast, ma'am?"

"No breakfast."

"Not even after helping you back there?"

"I didn't need you."

Crownover did not speak again. He watched her face, saw the determination and suspicion there, and he waited until a shading of expression passed over her features and the tough-set firmness of her mouth changed a little. Then he smiled.

"I didn't take you to be as hard as you talk, ma'am." He started forward. The trail was narrow, and she had either to precede him to the house or step aside. She preceded him. But at the hitch rail, while he tied the horse, she said sharply from under the porch overhang: "I didn't see anything funny."

He finished loosening the latigo and went toward her on the porch. "You weren't behind you," he said, the smile returning, widening until Crownover's teeth shone whitely.

"What do you mean by that, stranger?"

"I'm no stranger, ma'am. I told you my name. It's Burt Crownover. Well, what I meant by that was . . . I've never seen a woman in man's hide-britches before, and, followin' you down here . . . it just sort of tickled me is all."

She whirled away, dark blood sweeping upward from her throat. At that moment a large, heavy man opened the door, ignored the girl who fled past him, and fastened a genial, interested, and raffish look on Crownover. When he spoke, there was a quick lift of surprise to his tone.

"Well, stranger, figured you were someone else. Welcome, anyway. We're just fixing to have breakfast. Care to join us?"

"I'd like to very much," Crownover said. "Can I fork my animal some hay?"

The heavy man flagged, barnward. "Help yourself. I'll set another place." He looked beyond Crownover toward the creek path. He frowned faintly, then shrugged and turned inward beyond the door.

The heavy man's name was Abel Benton. The girl was his daughter and her name was Sue. They owned a grazing section in Rain Valley and wintered their cattle in the lowlands beyond the mountains Crownover had recently crossed, using the same trail to get out of the valley that Crownover had used to get in.

The girl did not reappear until her father had called twice. When she arrived, she wore a dress, and avoided Crownover's frankly admiring gaze with a degree of silent hostility that seemed to fill the log house.

Her father did not notice it, or, if he did, he ignored it. When they were sitting down, he said: "Birch was here. I sent him along to help you fetch water. Odd he isn't back yet."

The girl shot Crownover a flashing look when she replied. "I don't think he'll be back. This man knocked him down."

Abel Benton's fork hung in midair. "Hit Birch Walton?" he said. Benton turned this over in his mind and studied Crownover. "Why?" he finally asked.

Burt looked at the girl, waiting.

She hesitated a long time. "He wanted me to go to Brown's Hole with him and I didn't want to go." Abel Benton and Burt Crownover waited. There was an uncomfortable atmosphere around the table. "He grabbed me," the girl blurted swiftly. "He wouldn't let go, and this man came up behind us and knocked him down."

Benton said nothing until he had finished breakfast, then he got up and beckoned Crownover to follow him outside. When they were alone on the porch, Benton worked with a sculptor's elaborate attention over a brown-paper cigarette. He lit up and exhaled with his severe and troubled eyes on Crownover.

"Mister, you're just passin' through I take it."

"That's right."

"Well, then, seems to me you hadn't ought to have hit Birch Walton because, after you're gone, we got to live with him."

Crownover kept silent through a long, slow study of Sue Benton's father, then in a low drawl he said:

"You know, I've always sort of resented men who manhandle womenfolk. And if I were you, Mister Benton, I don't think I'd want much to do with a feller who acts like that."

"Well, now, son, you don't understand. Birch does me lots of favors. He sort of watches my cattle when he's ridin' and he . . ."

"Feeds the cow to get the calf," Crownover said dryly. "There's nothing new about that."

"Birch's not a bad feller, Mister Crownover." Benton's gaze drew out and his voice thickened. "And he's known in the valley as the fastest gun throughout these mountains."

Crownover swept the towering, upended world of Rain Valley's emptiness and said: "Might not be too much competition up here, Mister Benton. This is pretty isolated country."

Benton exhaled a bluish smoke cloud and half smiled. "You'd be surprised how many folks are in the valley. In about four miles there're three other outfits, not countin' mine or Birch Walton's place." Benton's gaze was fully on Crownover when he added: "If you hadn't come over the trail in the night, mister, you'd have never been able to slip up 'n' surprise anyone, either."

Crownover heard suspicion in Benton's tone, but only half heeded it. He looked for a moment up along the mountainside where the Rain Valley trail was, then swung his gaze abruptly against the older man. "You keep a sentinel up there?" he asked. Benton nodded and said no more; he was obviously waiting for something. Finally Crownover made a cigarette of his own, and, while his head was averted, he said: "Mighty pretty valley at that."

"Yes, it is."

"You got a match?"

"Sure."

"Thanks." Crownover inhaled deeply; there was the strong sweep of smoke into his lungs. "I guess a man could find a place to camp hereabouts."

"I guess he could," Benton conceded, still waiting.

"Tell me, Mister Benton, that sentry you put up on the mountaintop . . . he warns you folks when anyone's coming?"

"Uses a heliograph mirror, Mister Crownover. Hasn't a soul got past him ever . . . except you . . . and you sort of sneaked past, like maybe you knew he was up there . . . or else like you didn't want anyone beyond the mountains to see you crossin' the country."

Crownover did not give the answer Benton was waiting for. He was silently thoughtful again. Up the mountain was the barely discernible twisting and turning of the trail. It was wide, ankle-deep in dust, and, he recalled, smelling strongly of cattle. The longer he stood there thinking, the more a fixed idea firmed up in his mind.

Finally Benton cut across his preoccupation with: "We could set a spell, Mister Crownover."

They sat, smoking silently, with new-day warmth turning Rain Valley's thin air fragrant with pine scent, then Crownover asked quietly how Rain Valley got its name.

"Oh," replied Benton with little interest, "I expect because we get lots of spring and fall rains, but I don't know exactly."

"Up in Wyoming there's a valley sort of like this," Crownover said.

"Is there for a fact?"

"Yep. It's got a pretty fair trail into it now, but a

few years back it was isolated, too. Folks call it Rustler's Roost."

Benton's eyes sparkled. "That's a good name!" he exclaimed, pushing out short, massive legs and looking at them. He was obviously going to say more—it was apparent in the expression of his eyes and the shape of his mouth—but at that moment Sue came out onto the porch. Abel looked upward, letting his words quietly die.

She threw an intent look at Crownover. "I thought you were going to ride on," she said, forcing a hostility that rang false.

Crownover saw that she wore a split riding skirt and that her wealth of red-gold hair was caught up severely at the base of her neck with a small green ribbon. He tried to judge her and had a bad time of it. She was not a soft girl, he thought, not in the sense that most girls were soft, and there was something moving in the gold-flecked depths of her eyes. He could see it, but could not define it—resentment? anger? hostility? He sighed.

"My horse hasn't finished his hay yet, ma'am," he answered, "but I'll be out of your way shortly."

The girl flicked a look past at her father. "I'm going over to Springtime Meadow and see how the horses are." Abel nodded.

From the corner of his eye, Crownover saw the fat man's indulgence spread entirely over his face.

Sue did not move. Silence came down and stretched out thinly. When Crownover thought he could hear his own heart sloshing in the hush, without looking around at him, Sue said: "You can come along, if you like. There are fresh horses in the corral." Then she hastened around the cabin and faded from sight.

Crownover did not move at once. He slowly raised his head to gaze at Abel. "What caused that?" he inquired simply.

"Search me," Benton replied, looking even more surprised than Crownover. "But if you're in no great hurry, you might humor her a mite."

Crownover "humored" her. They rode silently, northwesterly, passing from tree shade to grassy parks and back to forested areas, traveling almost continually from bright sunlight to pleasant shadows. It was a two-hour ride before Sue Benton drew up on a little gravel knoll gazing down into a beautiful little landlocked meadow, perhaps five hundred acres in size, with a crooked creek working its way with difficulty through choking, stirrup-high grass. In the middle distance a band of horses, about thirty of them, grazed unconcernedly. Crownover swung down, studying the land beyond the park and behind them. He made a cigarette and watched the girl dismount, also. His expression was quizzical. In a totally dispassionate voice he said: "All right, Miss Sue, tell me."

"Tell you what?" she asked, her back to him, gazing down at the horses and the beautiful meadow beyond.

"One minute you could claw my eyes out. The next minute you invite me for a ride with you."

She dropped the reins and walked back into the shade near him, but facing partly away so that he could not see her face. He could, however, see her profile, the round curving of her shoulders and the fullness of her blouse still lower. Where filigreed sunlight spilled through pine limbs, her hair shone the dull, quenchless fire of old copper.

He thought her imperious now, until she spoke, then that illusion was shattered and she seemed like a very young girl full of trust and naïveté.

"I want you to stay, that's all."

"Why?" he asked, watching her and smoking, conscious of something disturbing there in the trees with them.

"You're just drifting, anyway."

"You know," he drawled, "my mother taught me to look at people when I talked to them."

She turned, throwing the full, strong power of her eyes against him, but, try as he might, he could read nothing there except that again he'd been wrong. She wasn't a very young girl, now, at all. She was a worldly woman rummaging his face for a key to his character, for signs of his weaknesses, and there was something about the way her mouth lay, gently closed and heavy, that fired rich longings in him.

"One place is as good as another, isn't it?" she asked. Then her tone turned sly. It reminded him of the look in Abel's eyes back on the porch. "No one ever comes to Rain Valley. A man could rest up here for months and never have to worry."

He smiled, and then he laughed, and she watched him from narrowing eyes. "Lady," he said, "Rain Valley isn't just the pretty hide-out it looks like, is it?"

"You could stay and find out, Mister Crownover."

"All right," he said easily, half smiling only and showing a challenge in his eyes and also a curiosity based on something hard and saturnine. "All right, Miss Sue, I'll stay. But I'm going to call you Sue, and you're going to call me Burt." His smile turned completely mirthless now. "And I'm not staying because you're pretty or because you want me to . . . because you don't care whether it's me or the next stranger who rides in."

She accepted his terms and continued to look up. "All right, Burt. But you might get to like it here."

He grunted, probing her for a hint of thoughts. "I might. And again I might turn out like your Birch Walton. Unless, of course, there are prettier girls in Rain Valley."

"There are," she said matter-of-factly. "You'll meet them."

Latent mirth showed again when he said: "Naw, Sue. There might be prettier ones, but, I reckon, I'll just sort of hang close to you. Know why?"

She shook her head without speaking and turned partly away from him.

"Well, a few days back on the trail I woke up and be dog-goned if in the night I hadn't grown three little rattlers on the end of my tailbone, which, of course, shows that I'm mean." He dropped the cigarette and stomped on it. "As mean as you are, Sue, and in time I'll learn to be as treacherous, too."

When she swung toward him, Crownover was toeing into the stirrup. He flung her a smile as he settled over the saddle. "Come on," he said carelessly, "let's get back. You've accomplished what you had in mind when you brought me up here, and I'm getting hungry again."

CHAPTER TWO

Crossing the last spit of trees before emerging in front of the cabin, Sue drew up sharply. Crownover, following the direction of her eyes, saw Abel talking to three lounging riders on the porch.

"Friends?" he asked.

"Don't you recognize the one in the blanket coat?"

Crownover looked again. "Your friend, Birch Walton," he murmured, then studied Walton's companions. "Who're the other ones?"

"That tall one is Dave Beck. The other one is Ed Roberts. They run with Birch a lot." Sue looked around. "You didn't think Birch would forget that, did you?"

He didn't reply.

Moments later they left the trees and started forward in plain sight. While they were still beyond hearing distance, Sue said: "Be careful what you say."

Crownover, studying the men on the porch who

were turning now, watching them approach, said: "I will be. I don't like the odds, either."

"It's not the odds," retorted Sue. "Ed and Dave won't pick a fight with you . . . not this time, anyway. What's bothering them is who you are and why you came into the valley like you did . . . in the night."

Abel boomed a hearty greeting as they rode up and got down. Crownover thought he was overdoing it and looked past where the lounging cattlemen were studying him from granite-still eyes. Only Birch Walton's face, stained with dark blood, showed anything at all.

"Mister Crownover, that there's Dave Beck, a good neighbor of our'n, and this here is Ed Roberts. Ed runs cows in Rain Valley, too." Abel's heartiness dwindled. He shifted his weight, and said quickly: "An' this is Birch Walton . . .'nother neighbor. Come on up on the porch out of the sun. Sue, honey . . . any coffee left?"

"I'll see," she said, and went as far as the door where she turned, looked at Crownover momentarily, then disappeared.

Dave Beck was a tall, well-built man with very light-colored eyes and a solid chin. Roberts seemed less positive, more amenable to compromise, to tolerance, and yet, beyond the façade of his gray stare, there seemed to be something constantly moving, something almost sly. He grinned at Burt, the only man on the porch to show friendliness except Abel Benton, and Abel was frankly uncomfortable.

With no preliminary, Dave Beck said: "Abel's been tellin' us about you, Mister Crownover, and it isn't really any of our business, but we're curious about why you came over the pass in the night."

This one, Crownover thought, would never shoot a man in the back, and, if he didn't like someone, the first person to know it would be the person he disliked. It might be that he would never like Dave Beck, but he could understand him, which is more than he could say for Birch Walton and the sly-smiling man seated beside Birch. When he answered, he looked fully at Beck.

"I got in the habit of doing that years back when there were still bronco bucks around."

Beck's eyes were disbelieving, but he made no contradiction while he let his gaze go boldly from Crownover's boots to his hat. "That brand on your horse," he eventually said, "it's not from this county."

"It's not even from this state," Burt said. "It's from Idaho, Mister Beck."

"You from Idaho, Mister Crownover?"

"No." Burt let it hang a moment. "I'm from Colorado. From Cache Le Poudre, Colorado. My name's Burt Crownover. I cut through these mountains on my way south."

"Where south?"

"Arizona, Mister Beck."

They all heard Crownover's voice turn thin-edged. Abel Benton cleared his throat, spat out into the yard, and looked worriedly around at the door.

Ed Roberts made a cigarette and held the sack toward Burt. He declined, and Roberts said: "There're shorter ways to get south of here than over the mountains, Mister Crownover. Back at Sageland you could've followed the stage road."

"Unless," Birch Walton cut in, giving Crownover a bright, black stare, "he had reason not to travel the roads." Walton was wanting trouble—it was a light in his eyes and an ugliness in his expression for all to see. He drew off the cabin wall, waiting.

Crownover turned away from him with a studied, a calculated movement, and faced Beck again. "I had a reason for cutting through the mountains, instead of trailing down the road . . . sure. But it concerns none of you, and we're going to leave it like that."

Beck said nothing. His eyes were judging, appraising, frankly calculating. He shoved up out of the chair and shrugged, then he said to Walton and Roberts as though the matter no longer interested him: "You fellers going up to Brown's Hole or not?"

Roberts also arose. He was still faintly smiling behind his cigarette, the blandness lingering in his expression. "I am," he told Beck, and started down off the porch.

"Birch?" Beck said.

Walton's head was tipped hawk-like toward Crownover. "Sure," he said in a voice gone soft, "but first I got this to do. . . ." He went forward in a coiled spring, and Crownover had no time to step back or twist away before Walton's fist caught him under the ear with terrific force. Crownover went backward off the porch and landed hard in the dust. He rolled over, got to all fours, and hung there, head down and resisting unconsciously the urge to collapse. Through a roaring he heard Walton say: "Now we're even." The ground reverberated with a diminishing sound as three horses loped away.

Abel grunted under Crownover's weight. He panted and cursed until he had the burden back on the porch, sprawled in a chair, then he said: "Mister Crownover, you got to watch yourself in Rain Valley."

* * *

Those were the words that remained in Crownover's mind after full consciousness returned. He was gingerly exploring the lump along his jaw when Sue came out with a tray and coffee. He dropped his hand as though nothing had happened, and the three of them drank silently, then Crownover said he was going to check his horse, and walked off. While Sue watched him go, Abel shook his head.

"I don't know, honey," he mused, "if he's ridin' the back trails or not, but I'll tell you this . . . him and Birch're goin' to tangle real good one of these days."

"What happened?" asked Sue.

Abel told her, then hoisted himself up out of the chair, and went as far as the door before he faced around. "Why did you take him with you this morning?" he asked mildly.

Sue put her cup aside. "We need him, Pa. We're only kidding ourselves about the cattle."

Abel considered this a moment. "But he's a drifter, honey."

"He'll stay."

"They usually don't, honey. I've seen hundreds of 'em come and go in my time." Abel's face softened; the raffishness left it to be replaced with a tinge of wistfulness. "You've only known him four, five hours, Sue. Don't go buildin' any dreams."

"Pa, there's something about him. . . ."

Abel's softening gaze quickened with fresh life. "What d'you mean?"

She got up, lifted the tray, and moved toward the door with it. "I don't know. It puzzles me."

"Well now, Daughter," Abel began in a fading tone, "'most any young buck is handsome when they're his age."

"It's not that," Sue said, flaring an annoyed look at her father. "It's something else. He's acts so confident . . . so graceful the way he moves. . . ."

"Didn't look very graceful to me when Birch dropped him."

"You're not trying to understand," Sue said shortly, and edged past into the cabin.

Abel padded after her into the kitchen. "Yes, I am, honey."

"Watch him, Pa. Watch the way he moves . . . the way he keeps his eyes moving. It's got nothing to do with his looks, at all."

Abel rubbed his jaw. He studied Sue's back, then went forward and peered through a window, barnward. "I think," he finally said in a very quiet tone, "he's an outlaw. Like I said on the porch . . . he told Dave he come into the mountains for a reason." He wagged his head. "An' you be careful around him, too. No tellin' what he's like inside."

Sue looked up from the sink. "I know what he's like inside, Pa. He's like every other man God ever made *that* way. But that doesn't worry me. He's not like Birch."

Abel started out of the kitchen. "All right," he said with resignation, "only I bet he'll ride on."

"I can make him stay, Pa."

Abel stopped, but Sue was humming at the sink. She moved briskly at her work as though the subject was closed, and it was.

Abel considered—in so many ways she was like her mother, dead now these past seven years. There was the same iron streak in both of them. He started when boots struck down hard on the porch beyond, then scuttled forward. "Come on in!" he called, and beamed when Crownover entered. "Sue's fixin' some dinner . . . it'll be along directly."

Crownover stopped just inside the door. His shoulder points nearly reached to each side of the opening. "I think I'll go for a little ride," he said. That and no more.

Abel searched his face. "Well, sure, boy, only dinner'll be ready in a few minutes. Ridin' can wait when there's eatin' to be done." He smiled.

"I'll eat later," Crownover said, and left the house, crossed to the hitch rail, stepped aboard his horse, and reined away.

Abel went to the door and watched him a moment then called: "Sue, come here!" After she was there beside him, Abel said: "He had a real strange look on his face. You expect he's goin' after Birch?"

Sue balled up her apron, thrust it into her father's hands, and went through the door without answering. She was halfway to the barn when he called to her: "Where you going? Who's goin' to fix dinner?"

"You are," she said, and hastened into the barn, emerged moments later astride a chestnut mare, and loped easily, northwesterly into the trees.

Abel considered the apron. He punched it into a pocket and started for the kitchen with a mumble of indulgent resignation.

Beyond the Benton place, across the creek with its glass-clear water and immaculate gravel, the Rain Valley trail began its deceptively gradual descent, but less than a quarter mile ahead there was a dim second trail that threw itself upward and over a quick, sharp rise, then followed land contours westerly where the bend of mountains drew back toward the north. It was this second trail Burt Crownover rode now, and it was cooler in here where giant pines flared upward hundreds of feet, their red-bark trunks thicker than a horse was long. The air was thin, scented, and faintly reddened. Where an occasional small clearing was crossed by the trail, Burt could see the far-off peaks and saddles, the thick spruce stands, and occasionally a snow field nestled in some crevice. The sky overhead was blue-faded and a little brassy where it dim-merged with the horizon. There was not a sound coming through to him—not even the footfalls of his own mount that trod matted pine needles with a wise sure-footedness. There was nothing as treacherous as pine needles to a horse wearing uncaulked shoes, but the only horses that knew that were the ones who were mountain-wise.

There was a little taste of dust in the air, not really strong enough to be noticed unless a man sniffed for it. But it was there and it meant someone had recently passed along the trail ahead of Crownover. When the taste got stronger two hours later, Crownover pulled off the trail, rode deeper into the forest, and dismounted. Let the dust settle. Let the riders making it get farther ahead. Crownover walked idly along an elk trail and came out upon a sudden drop-off. Five hundred feet below, shaped like a frying pan, was a volcanic lake. Beyond the lake, spreading out circularly, was a mountain meadow that faded out where mountain flanks came down to darken it with their shadows. Beneath trees during this hottest part of the day were cattle, some standing, some lying down, a few grazing out where wildflowers splashed color against the grass.

Crownover made a cigarette, squatted on his spurs, and smoked. The sun was reddening, falling gently westward and a large, lazy white cloud passed along, trailing its shadow over the meadow and the fry-pan lake. There was no need to go farther; he knew without returning to the trail that he had found Brown's Hole.

By sitting there leisurely Crownover could distinguish the distant trail where it showed against forest and stone, winding distantly downward to the meadow, cutting in and out of trees and shadows and lower, shiny-trunked manzanita bushes.

He picked up the horsemen, too, doll-size and moving slowly out onto the meadow. Three of them. He watched them work through the cattle, stopping here and there, probably talking, making infrequent gestures, and continuing on toward the lake until they were almost directly beneath his elk-trail upthrust. He recognized the men by their shapes when they dismounted, moving closer to the water, edging into tree shade to stop together.

He stood up and went farther back from the rim, then he continued to gaze into the meadow a moment. Finally, looking skyward, he saw the faint haze of early evening, the far-off changing colors on the mountainsides, and started back toward the trail, still walking beside the horse, thinking private thoughts.

He stepped across the saddle with his horse reversed and rode back the way he had come. In among the trees, darkness seemed never to have lifted, but only to have begrudgingly brightened through the nooning hours. By the time he was back at the creek, smoke-hazed evening was down and the heat rolled back to leave a settling drowsiness, a stillness as heavy and tangible as lead.

He thought once, before obscurity came, that he saw fresh horse tracks on the ground ahead, but no one had passed him on the trail and certainly the men he had followed had not gotten ahead of him. He decided it was an illusion and rode all the way back to Benton's barn at a slow walk. There, he off-saddled, forked hay, then crossed through the dusk to the front porch.

Abel was sitting there. So, also, was Sue. They seemed inward, scarcely looking at him long enough to make greetings. He dropped into a chair and blew out a long breath. "Sure is peaceful in here," he said.

Abel nodded. "Have a nice ride?"

"Yeah. Went out through the trees across the creek a ways, and back again."

Sue struck her boot with a braided quirt and got up. "I'll get supper," she said, avoiding Crownover's eyes, and passed into the house.

"Didn't run into Beck and Roberts and Walton did you?" asked Abel.

"No."

"Funny. They took the Brown's Hole trail, too."

A warning ran out along Crownover's nerves. He continued, relaxed and motionless, moments longer, then he said: "I've got a feeling you need someone to ride for you. Am I right?"

"Well, I could use a man, all right," conceded Abel, "only I'm just a small rancher an' you know how that is . . . can't pay big-outfit wages."

"Maybe we could work something out."

Abel turned this over in his mind, reached some kind of conclusion, then changed the subject. "Hattie Richmond came by while you was gone."

"Hattie Richmond?"

"A neighbor. Her husband's Rich Richmond, runs cattle in the valley. Hattie's worked up a social for Saturday night."

Crownover's mind cut past Abel's dissembling, struck what he thought was the core of an idea in the other man's mind, and waited. But what Abel might have said was forever stilled by Sue calling them to supper. They trooped inside, ate in a silence Crownover thought foreign to both Bentons, and afterward he helped Sue clear the table and do the dishes.

Somewhere not too far from the cabin a wolf barked hungrily. Farther out it got an answer. "Ought to be good hunting in Rain Valley," Crownover said.

"There is," came the answer, brusque and to the point.

"Good riding country, too."

Sue sluiced the dishpan with dippered water and said nothing.

Crownover stacked dishes. "Why did you follow me today?" he asked quietly.

She turned on him. "Who said I did?"

"Your pa. Not in so many words, but he knew which trail I took."

"Maybe it was him."

Crownover faced around, shaking his head. "You know better. I've only been here one day and I know better, too. Your pa doesn't ride a hundred yards from this cabin unless he has to." He waited.

Sue dried her hands, crossed to a hanging mirror, and ran both hands under her hair. She was looking back at him in the shadowy lamplight. Her reserve was thawing, he could see that. It was as though she needed someone to talk to, someone to confide in who she might trust. He knew she had not yet reached a judgment concerning him, but for some reason—and it was more than ever obvious now—she had to talk to someone. "All right, it was me," she said.

"Why, Sue?"

"I thought you might be after Birch Walton."

"With those other two with him?"

She swung around. "How did I know . . . maybe a bush-whack on the trail."

He draped the damp dishcloth over an edge of the drain board before speaking again. "All right. And when you saw that wasn't what I had in mind . . . then what?"

"I came back."

"I didn't mean that. I meant what did you think, then?"

"It doesn't matter." Her shoulders slumped. "Are you going to stay on like you said?"

"Sure. You know that. Don't change the subject."

She kept her eyes on his face, and it was very clear to Crownover that she wanted to trust him and could not. "I thought . . . why is he sitting there like that, watching them ride the cattle trail?"

It was his turn to change the conversation's course and he did. "Was that Brown's Hole?"

"Yes."

"Who owns all those cattle down there?"

"All of us. Everyone in the valley turns out in there."

He crossed to the doorway. "Sue?"

"Yes."

"You going to Richmond's social with Walton?"

"He hasn't asked me yet."

"Will you go with me?"

"Yes."

He continued to watch her face, profiled to him.

"It's been a long time since I've had a woman show such enthusiasm about going to a social with me," he said, then went on through the house and out onto the porch. Abel was asleep in a chair with night's warm darkness dropping on him from the porch overhang.

Crownover stepped into the dust and strode directly toward the barn. He thought that Sue did not think he intended to bushwhack Birch Walton at all. Trailing him had to do with her uncertainty of him, her perplexity and suspicion.

He walked to the corral and, there, hung on the bars, smoking. Beyond in the very faint starshine, Benton's horses made snuffling sounds among the mangers. There was a good scent of cooling earth and horse sweat in the night. Overhead, a new moon, scimitar-curved and coldly silver, cast downward its palest reflection. Crownover watched the house until his cigarette was finished, then he slowly turned and traced out against the dark horizon sharp outlines of mountains where they stood blacker in the night.

He continued to stand like that for nearly an hour, thinking that Sue could be dangerous, that he would earn her confidence between now and the social, and that, if he could not do it, then he would have to grow a third eye in the back of his head. He was still thinking like that when a pebble dropped at his feet, then another one, and finally from the darkness a voice said: "Over here by the barn. The north side."

He did not move at once, but threw outward and forward a steady, searching gaze. Then he passed into darkness fading out toward the barn, and, when he could distinguish the thin wedge of man shape, he said: "Have any trouble?"

The shadow answered softly: "Not a bit. But I know where their sentry camps on the peak."

Crownover squatted. The vague man shape also hunkered down. "Where are you camped?" Crownover asked.

"Mile or so west of here, with my back to the hills."

"You see that big valley with the cattle in it?"

"Yeah, I'm camped against the foothills at the north end of it. Are those the critters, you reckon?"

Crownover nodded. "So far I haven't run across any others in the valley, but we've got plenty of time."

"Be a helluva job gettin' them back out of here over that trail without being seen and jumped by every man in here."

"There's no big hurry," Crownover reiterated. "Listen, Jake, today I met three fellers . . . Dave Beck, Birch Walton, Ed Roberts. Remember those names."

"All right. Trouble?"

"Yes, particularly Beck and Walton. Walton's supposed to be handy with a gun. If you run into him and there's trouble . . . shoot. Don't wait, just shoot."

"All right." The vague shadow straightened up. "Anything else?"

Crownover came upright, too. "Not right now, no."

"*Adiós*, then."

"*Adiós*."

Crownover waited until the unseen silhouette melted into gloom with an atrophying sound of leather against leather, then he went to the front of the barn and stood there, taking the pulse of the night.

Across the yard Abel Benton's log house was square-etched in darkness; beyond it the forested fingerlings of trees thrust hard against a serene sky and Rain Valley was steeped in hush and stillness. He turned finally, entered the barn, climbed to the loft, and unrolled blankets in the chaff, kicked off his boots, cast aside his hat, lay his gun close by, and settled back, thinking of Sue, Birch Walton, Dave Beck, Ed Roberts, and Abel Benton. But mostly of Sue.

CHAPTER THREE

Crownover rode twice in the next three days to Brown's Hole with Sue Benton. Each time she pointed out the different brands. The last time they rode over, Friday, before the social at Richmond's ranch, she brought a cloth-wrapped lunch that they ate in the shade beside the clear-water, fry-pan lake, and Crownover thought he had finally earned her trust.

She said: "You're like the others, aren't you?"

And he knew he had, once again, misjudged her.

"What do you mean?"

"Watchful, secretive, careful what you say."

There was disappointment in her expression that he noted and felt keenly. "That's the way a man becomes," he murmured.

"If he's an outlaw, yes. Otherwise, no. There's no reason for a man to be that way if he has nothing to hide."

Crownover finished eating, made a cigarette, and lit up. He eased back against a tree and watched cloud shapes follow the overhead curve of heaven. "You're betting money I'm an outlaw," he said. "I guess living up here alone makes folks suspicious."

"Only when strangers ride in," she threw at him, "like you did . . . in the night."

"I told your friends I was passing through."

"But you stayed here."

He looked down into her face. "Sue, you asked me to."

"Oh, stop it!" she exclaimed. "You know that's not why you stayed."

"All right. Why did I agree to stay?"

"I don't know, but I wish I did."

He watched her face grow troubled again. "Then I'll ride on." He got up, struck his trousers with his hat, and held out a hand.

She ignored it, got up by herself, and started toward their horses. From the saddle she said: "No. I want you to stay."

Crownover looked over the meadow at the cattle darkening its greenness and lifted his reins. "Which is worse," he asked, "being careful in a new country like I am, or holding things back like you are doing?"

She started ahead toward the trail and he followed her in silence until they were leaning into the spiraling incline, then he called forward: "Sue? You don't have to change your opinion of me. You don't have to put on this act, either, so I'll stay and help Abel. But if I'm going to help, don't you think I ought to know what's going on?"

She neither looked back nor answered.

They rode all the way back to the creek before either of them spoke again, then, as Sue's horse dropped its head to drink noisily around the bit, she said: "The last two nights you've ridden out . . . where did you go?"

Crownover's eyes lost their warmth. They drew out narrowly in a steady regard of her. "How do you know that?" he asked.

"The sheep pelt on your saddle skirts was wet morning before last, and again yesterday morning." She pulled the horse's head up.

"Wait a minute, Sue," Crownover said in a low voice. "A thing like that can rile a man."

She swung hard toward him, and she too had a temper—it showed in the flare of her nostrils and the hot-fire points in her eyes. It was also evident in her two-edged tone of voice. "What did you expect me to do . . . sit and wonder about you? I'm not made that way." Her anger faded. "Yes," she said, "I'll tell you what's wrong . . . when you tell me where you went those nights and why you sat up there watching Birch and Roberts and Dave Beck . . . and why you sneaked into the valley in the night in the first place." She waited, watching his face with attentive regard.

For the second time since his arrival in Rain Valley, Crownover felt a warning run out along his nerves. He shifted in the saddle; he looked beyond the trees where the Benton cabin sat and where sunshine lay, orange-yellow, upon the open country, changing it without ever changing the forest that fringed it.

"Well?" she demanded.

"I explored the valley," he said, all trace of anger gone. "I scouted around looking up the other ranches, getting the lay of the land." He looked at her. "Is that some sort of crime?"

"Maybe. Why did you do it in the night?"

"You never let up do you? I did it in the night because, as suspicious as you Rain Valley people are, if I'd done it in daylight, I'd have had Beck and Roberts and Walton and the Lord knows who else, all runnin' over here, questioning me again." He paused. "And I'm getting a little tired of folks' nosy curiosity."

Sue digested this, and from beneath his lashes Crownover saw her plain wish to believe him, and her fear to do so. She tossed her head to push back hair and she looked up quickly when a tree squirrel peeped around a tree trunk from twenty feet off the ground to watch them. Finally she said—"We'll talk tomorrow night."—and all the sharpness was gone from her voice. She looked back at him. "Is that all right?"

"Sure, Sue. We'd better get along."

Abel had the wood stove going. He was frying meat and wild greens when Sue and Crownover entered the kitchen, side-by-side. He smiled and asked about the cattle. Sue told him in an absent way that they looked fine. She was subdued and scarcely spoke the balance of that evening and the next day, when Crownover went back to Brown's Hole with a pack animal and six gunny sacks of hard salt for the cattle. She profited from his absence by taking a tub bath and spending the rest of the day working on a dress.

Late in the afternoon Abel got out the top buggy, brought over the mountains years before piece by piece, dusted it off, and checked the driving harness. He seemed pleased—more so than usual, although by nature he was a smiling man, not soft or easy, but certainly lazy and good-natured. But Abel Benton

also possessed that peculiar wariness in his gaze
Crownover had noticed in the men of Rain Valley.

It was nearing sundown when Sue crossed the
yard to stop where her father was working on the
buggy with a very faint frown marring her forehead. "He should've been back by now," she said.

Abel cast her a slow look. "Well, now, honey," he
soothed, "it takes a while to get over there. He had
to put out those sacks of salt."

She was looking mountainward, still with the little frown. "He's been gone all day, Pa. It doesn't take
that long."

"It's warm today," Abel stated. "Maybe he stripped
down and cooled off in the lake." Abel straightened
up; he leaned on the buggy, watching his daughter's
face. "Sue?" She turned. "Honey, there's nothing to
get all upset about."

"I'm not upset!"

Abel's eyebrows went upward. "You're not? Well,
you sure fooled me." He smiled. "He'll be along . . .
go on back to the house and get dressed. He hasn't
seen you spruced up yet."

"I don't care about that, Pa. I just keep. . . ."

"No," Abel said gravely, watching his daughter's
troubled expression. "I'm sure you don't. But all the
same he'll be surprised, I bet. You look pretty as a
mornin' sunrise when you're ready for a social."

Very gradually understanding came to Sue. Her
eyes widened. "Pa . . . !"

"Well, now, honey, he's a likely lad. I like him better'n Birch, and I can tell he likes you."

"How can you tell?" she asked in a quick tone.

Abel's smile grew and spread and his eyes were
shrewd.

"It's not hard when you've lived as long as I have. I can see you sort of like him, too, honey."

"I'm afraid of him," Sue said breathlessly.

Abel showed surprise. "Afraid?" he echoed. "How?"

Sue turned. "Not that way, Pa. Not physically. I'm afraid that he'll turn out . . ." She never finished.

Abel watched her run across the yard and disappear into the cabin. He scratched his belly, turned, and leaned on the buggy, gazing narrowly toward the mountains that stood solidly banked against the western sky.

Crownover rode into the Benton yard with dusk half masking the forest at his back. He put up the horses and walked into the barn. Abel was there in the gloom, sitting on a keg, chewing straw. He had on a coat and was freshly shaven. "Make out all right?" he asked.

"Fine," Crownover said, continuing on past toward the loft ladder.

"Took quite a spell, though."

Crownover, with one hand on the ladder, turned and looked down at Benton. "I didn't hurry."

"I see that." Abel arose, brushed the seat of his trousers, and started toward the doorway. "Better hurry now, Sue's ready an' we don't want to be late."

Crownover, sensing something veiled in Abel's words, climbed slowly upward. He changed his clothing, came back down, scrubbed himself at the wash rack, and went out into the yard. Sue and her father were already in the buggy. Crownover crossed over and climbed in. Without a word, Abel started forward.

The trail to Richmond's ranch was strong with settling dust. Long before they broke out of the last trees, music came down the night to them and, closer, the sounds of laughter and activity, squeaking rigs, stomping horses, and unoiled saddlery.

Crownover was surprised, when they swerved at last into the yard, at the number of people. They stood in groups or moved swiftly under lantern light, scrubbed faces shiny and excited. The men were cattlemen and dressed in the attire of their trade; some, the older men particularly, wore long, nearly knee-length frock coats and every hat had been carefully brushed clean of every mark but sweat stains.

As they were getting down, Crownover saw three very pretty girls. They were watching the Bentons. Crownover gave them a long look. A voice beside him said—"I told you there were prettier ones."— then Sue moved past with her father and dead ahead, coming out of a group of younger men, Birch Walton crossed to them with his black gaze strong on Sue and his full lips closed and unsmiling. He cast Crownover only one quick glance.

"First dance?" Walton asked.

Sue said—"Not the first nor the last, Birch."—and moved on.

The dark man's gaze sought Crownover again, and this time it lingered.

Inside, Abel introduced Crownover around. He met Dave Beck's grave nod with a bow equally as silent and formal. He exchanged the same cool smile with Ed Roberts. When he met Rich Richmond, a short, paunchy, little man with weak, wet eyes behind thick spectacles, a downward mouth lipless and bloodless, and a short, almost unnaturally snubbed nose, he gripped the man's fat little hand and felt repelled by Richmond's ruthless and reptilian gaze.

Sue came up for the first dance, and Crownover glimpsed Birch Walton drinking surreptitiously from a furtively passed bottle among the younger men just beyond the doorway. In a corner of his mind Crownover considered the possibility of Walton's causing trouble, then Sue was speaking to him.

"They want to be introduced to you," she said.

Crownover looked down at her. "Who?"

"Who? Those girls you were staring at, who else?"

"Sue?"

"What?"

"I don't want to meet them especially."

She looked beyond him at other dancing couples. Her face, he thought, was unnaturally white—either that or her eyes, darkened in this light, seemed too large for the rest of her features.

Nonetheless, he met the girls and danced with each of them, and, while he was occupied, Sue's gaze bored into him. He felt it even when she whirled by on Birch Walton's arm or the arm of some other young cowman, making it a point not to see him at all.

Near midnight there was a pause in the music, but not in the noise, while everyone trooped outside to laden tables and ate. Abel joined Crownover beneath a red fir tree and said: "Richmond's been askin' around about you."

"What of it?" Crownover said, looking for Sue in the dim light and constant movement.

"Well, Richmond's just about the biggest cowman in the valley, boy."

Crownover continued eating and searching. Once

he thought he saw her with two other girls, but the crowd shifted and he lost her again.

"Aren't you impressed?" Abel asked with a side-long glance.

"Impressed as hell," Crownover growled.

"He could pay you good wages, boy. You're goin' to need good wages for a stake."

"What stake?" Crownover turned with a frown.

Abel put aside his plate and took up a tin cup. He did not reply until he had drained it and belched. "Well, a feller always needs a stake," he said evasively. Then he lowered his voice. "Dave's comin' this way."

Crownover did not look up until Beck's large shadow fell across them. He nodded, and Beck returned it. Behind him, an equally tall man but more raw-boned approached. The second man had a black moustache with upcurling, carefully tended corners, and his eyes were as black as midnight.

"Mister Crownover," Beck said, "this here is Dan Younger." When a handshake had been exchanged, Beck went on. "Dan's got a place adjoins mine south of Richmond's." Beck moved aside, and Dan Younger's black stare and unsmiling face came closer. "Abel," he said without looking away from Crownover, "there's a fresh jug of valley tan in my rig."

Abel left without a word, and Younger took his vacated seat. Dave Beck stood slouched against the red fir tree trunk and gazed out over the crowd.

"Crownover, we don't get many strangers in Rain Valley," Younger explained, half twisted forward and leaning a little. "So there's always room for a good hand in here." He waited, but Crownover said nothing. "You lookin' for a job by any chance?"

"No, I was ridin' through, but Abel said he could use me for a spell. I'm going to do a little work for him for the extra money and until my horse gets rested up."

"Then move on again?"

"That's right."

Younger leaned back. He shot Beck a look over Crownover's head, then crossed his legs and ran the back of one hand under his moustache. "Maybe you could make more money with less work and get a fresh horse thrown in," he said.

Crownover turned to face the dark man. "How?" he asked.

"Riding," Younger said, "but first . . . you got objections to tellin' me why you slipped into the valley in the night?"

Crownover felt Beck's gaze fully on him. He did not immediately reply, then he said: "Mister Younger, I'll put it this way. It's no one's damned business why I did that, but it's sure caused a lot of curiosity."

"Yes, it has," Younger agreed blandly. "You see, Mister Crownover, there's men in Rain Valley that'd just as soon not run into strangers." The black, bland eyes remained unwaveringly on Crownover. "Mind telling me why, now?'

"I'd just as soon not run into too many strangers myself. Does that answer you, Mister Younger?"

The raw-boned man inclined his head. "I think it does, Mister Crownover." He got up. "You think about that job a day or two, and, if you decide you'd be interested, come by my place."

Younger and Beck moved off. Crownover watched them cross to where Richmond stood, fat arms crossed high over his belly, waiting. The three men spoke briefly together, then drifted apart.

Sue came from around the tree and dropped down onto the seat Younger had vacated. Her face was colored from exertion. "I saw Pa," she said. "He told me you met Dan Younger."

"I did."

"What do you think of him?"

He shrugged, and after a thoughtful moment he said: "Sue, I think there's comin' a time when I'm going to wish I could trust you as much as you wish you could trust me."

She seemed to be considering this through the ensuing long moment of silence, then she said: "Maybe we ought to be getting along home."

He stood up. "I'll go find Abel," he said. But before he could move off, she touched his arm, after coming upright.

"You get the rig," she said. "I know where Pa is."

He did not go at once toward the row of buggies, but watched her cross the yard. Not until she was fully limned in lantern light did he notice her, then the strong hungers came up in him and for a while he saw nothing but Sue Benton's profiled figure where she stopped a moment to talk. He eventually passed along beyond the crowd, moving toward the buggies.

It was darker there with only a very faint light from the sky, softening outlines, and he did not see the dusty silhouettes until a voice came out to him.

"Crownover!"

He turned, suddenly alive to the shiny face there in the shadows, to the strong, gusty breath, and the tough-set jaw and mouth. He noted the other men, four of them, standing farther back in anticipation.

"What do you want, Walton?"

"I want to tell you something, Crownover. You

saddle up and ride on. You go tonight . . . right after you get back to Benton's. You understand me?"

"Yeah, I understand you."

Walton weaved closer. He smiled with his mouth the full width of his face, but his eyes were definitely not mirthful. His breath was foul with liquor scent. "All right, now get!"

"I said I understood you. I didn't say I was going to obey you."

Walton's wide smile faded, his face went forward, and one hand brushed back his coat to reveal the ivory-butted six-gun. "I'll kill you, Crownover. Goddamn you . . . I'll kill you."

"Not drunk you won't, Walton."

Crownover looked beyond at the still shapes. They were stone-like with anticipation, but none had made a move to uncover a gun. Behind them, beyond the rigs and drowsing animals, people moved across the Richmond yard, talking and laughing. There was a slight breeze swaying the lanterns.

"You fellows," Crownover said to the watching men, "are you buying in, too?"

A rough voice said: "No."

Crownover moved lightning-like then, and the crack of his fist made a meaty, sharp sound. Walton fell in a heap. Dust burst out around his flattened figure, and Crownover faced swiftly forward. None of the other men had moved. Silence settled suffocatingly and drew out over a full sixty seconds, then one of the dark shapes went to Walton and gazed downward.

"All right," he said tonelessly to Crownover. "I guess you could've killed him, mister."

The other men crowded up, too. One of them said:

"Maybe you should've, Crownover. Because now he'll kill you."

They picked Walton up and went in among the rigs with him.

At the buggy there was time to make a cigarette and partially smoke it before Sue and her father came along. By then Crownover's mood had changed from hard anger to remorse. Fighting with Birch Walton had no place in his private thoughts and could, conceivably, spoil what he had in mind.

He listened in total silence to Sue and Abel discuss the social all the way back to the ranch. At the barn he said he would put up the horse, and turned his back as they went slowly across the yard and into the house.

It took only a moment to throw the harness into Abel's rig and turn the horse loose. It walked a short way into the corral, dropped down with a solid grunt, and rolled first one way, then another. Crownover stood watching it, lost in his thoughts, and turned only when a faint rustling sound came to him.

It was Sue. She said: "I forgot to thank you."

He studied her, doubting very much that this was the only thing that had brought her back to the moonlighted yard. Ten feet away with starshine outlining each rise and fall of her breasts, each shadow that lay across her face and the almond-shaped eyes, obsidian now in the night, Crownover saw her as apart from everything in Rain Valley for this one moment and his powerful hungers returned. He went closer.

"You looked very pretty tonight, Sue."

"Thank you."

He reached out slowly, and she swayed toward

him. They came together, shadows blending in the pleasant gloom. He found her lips with no effort and, at first, pressed his mouth downward with tender pressure. But it was not enough, and she was overwhelmed with the fire that burnt against her, coming unchecked from him, until he held her away, saw the drained pallor of her face and the roundness of her eyes, and let his arms drop away.

"You didn't slap me," he said. "You didn't fight, Sue."

"No."

"Good night."

"Good night, Burt."

Where the high sky merged with Rain Valley's girding mountaintops, there was a corrugated band of paling light. It would soon be dawn.

How did you explain, in a woman, distrust for a man and passion for him at the same time? Burt did not know. He did not know, either, why he had let himself forget why he was in Rain Valley and kiss Abel Benton's daughter. His heart should have been singing. It was not.

CHAPTER FOUR

Crownover was shoeing his horse, morning sunlight splayed out through the trees in golden shafts that brightened everything, and overhead from the cabin was a milky drift of smoke from the kitchen.

Abel came out, sucking his teeth. He watched Crownover work for a while, then he said—"Let's you 'n' me ride out a little today."—and waited.

Crownover gathered the tools and started for the barn. When he reemerged, he had his saddle, blanket, and bridle.

Seeing this, Abel went to catch a horse. He said nothing more until they were going out through the trees. "You're kind of quiet this morning."

Crownover gave him a blank look. "Should I stand up on my hind legs and crow?" he asked.

Abel laughed and shook his head. He led the way, and, after they had crossed the creek, he did not, as Crownover expected, make for the Brown's Hole trail, but struck off into the forest northerly, hugging the slope as far as another dim trail. There he continued onward, humming to himself, fat bulk quivering gently along, pacing out the shadows even where there was no trail with a familiarity that left Crownover with no doubt but that he knew where he was going.

They rode steadily until the sun was directly above. Where the trees thinned out infrequently, the air was still and hot. Once, they surprised a small band of muletail deer; another time, although they never saw it, a bear went bumbling and whining up the mountain ahead of them, disturbed among some chokecherry bushes.

They were above the meadow and far past the frypan lake. Crownover could see that, but it only gradually came to him that Abel was heading for the far, barren mountain slope at the west end of Brown's Hole. He was a little suspicious, but more than that he began to sense a purpose behind Benton's long silence and his purposeful direction. When they passed over a shale rim and started downward, he spoke.

"Where are we going, Abel?"

"Down here a ways," the rancher replied easily, and Crownover knew without seeing that Abel was wearing his raffish smile.

"I guessed that, but what for?"

Now Abel turned in the saddle. "Well, I haven't been over in here for quite a time, and, seein' it's Sunday and all, I just figured I'd like to make the ride." His puckered eyes lingered on Crownover's face briefly, then he sat forward again and their mounts started fully downward into a gloomy cañon that ran out into the meadow. They were still a quarter mile from the mouth when Crownover smelled smoke. He was thinking of a way to detour

Abel when a horseman came up toward them. It was Dave Beck. He reined up and waited, watching them gravely and impassively.

"'Mornin'," he said, turned, and rode to the cañon's widening, and stopped. There, Crownover saw, sat Ed Roberts and Dan Younger. They exchanged solemn nods. Abel grunted down out of the saddle, rubbing his legs. Crownover did not dismount. Ahead of him, beyond where the others sat, were the remains of a cowboy camp. There was a stone ring for a cooking fire, peeled brush limbs where clothing and cooking utensils had hung, and across the earth, trampled by boot prints and horse sign, were tracks that the Rain Valley men had carefully avoided riding over.

Crownover, touched on a vulnerable nerve, held himself still, relaxed and impassive. The silence around him was oppressive, and, when he finally looked up, he found four sets of eyes regarding him with a clear and cold suspicion.

Abel, as usual, broke the stillness. "Been somebody camped up in here, looks like."

Dan Younger said—"Yeah."—so dryly it was almost a whisper. "Anybody know who it was?"

Crownover eased back against the cantle, looped the reins, and pushed back his hat. His expression turned frankly open with understanding. It was a good piece of acting. "You fellers don't know who was camped here?"

Two men shook their heads, two did not move at all except to join in looking squarely at the speaker.

"But you think because I'm a stranger that I'd know. Isn't that it?"

"We wondered," Beck said.

Crownover looked down at Abel. "Thanks," he said.

Abel spread his hands. "They asked me last night to fetch you along, Burt. Hell, no harm done, is there?"

"No, Abel, no harm done. But there could've been if I'd known anything about this."

"Don't you?" Dan Younger asked.

Crownover met the steady black stare. "No."

Younger looked at the trampled ground for a moment. "Wasn't anyone from the valley," he said, "we know that. So it had to be a stranger." His gaze lifted. "You're the only newcomer, Crownover . . . if you were in our place, what would you think?"

Crownover, too, studied the camp. As far as he could see, it could have been anyone's stopover, but, in a secret place of his mind, he reflected that the cowmen had obviously been here some time before he and Abel rode in. If they had found anything, it would be in someone's pocket now, and they would be waiting to trip him up with it.

He knew whose camp it was, of course. He also knew that whatever else the cowmen had found, they would not have found the camper because Jake Windsor was too old a hand to be ambushed. He said: "We could track him down."

Ed Roberts smiled. "We tried that. He went along the west end of the meadow, then up into the granite rock."

"Maybe he was just passing through," Crownover said.

Roberts still smiled. "Look at the ground. This feller's been in here at least four days, maybe longer. Another thing . . . a man riding through the mountains favors his horse." Roberts raised an arm and pointed with it southward. "This feller didn't ride across the meadow and out the far side, he cut along the edge of the grass and up into the granite country where he can't be tracked." The arm dropped. Roberts's genial face turned toward Crownover. "He was hiding . . . being careful not to be seen. He took the hardest, not the easiest, trail."

Crownover shrugged and threw a look at Dan Younger. "You said there are folks in here that'd just as soon stay out of sight."

Younger did not speak. He looked at the others. Silence settled among them. After a moment Dave Beck, who had been watching Crownover closely, got off his horse and went cat-footing it around the campsite.

"It might be," he mused, "like you said, Ed . . . an outlaw on the move."

Crownover masked the flooding relief by swinging down and going forward to squat and gaze at the tracks with his back to everyone but Dave Beck. It was harder to hide the relief than it had been to secret the alarm. Saddles squeaked behind him, spurred boots came softly forward, and Dan Younger hunkered nearby, took up a twig, and traced the outline of a boot, frowning. "It isn't who he is that bothers me so much as it's what he was doing here." He threw down the stick and swore. "Why would he camp here so long, just doing nothing?"

Crownover straightened up, letting his gaze run out along the western rims and cañons. "Could be a dozen reasons," he said. "A lame horse . . . tired out . . . been running . . . maybe even hurt." He shrugged.

Beck made a cigarette and smoked. Abel went

over against the cañon's low wall and dropped down to chew a twig and watch the others. Roberts watched Younger and Beck a moment, then faced toward Crownover.

"You can see how it is, can't you?" Roberts said.

"Sure, I can see. Only, if I'd been you fellers, I wouldn't have put on this play act."

"No?" Dave Beck said softly.

"No. I'd have gotten up a posse and put men at every buck trail leading out of here southward until I found him."

Beck inclined his head. "We did that," he said in the same soft tone. "Did it yesterday when one of Richmond's riders stumbled onto this camp." He was watching Crownover closely again. "Whoever he is, he won't get out of here now."

Roberts got back into his saddle and took up the reins. "I got to get back," he said pleasantly. "If any of you want me, I'll be at the ranch." He waited a moment, no one spoke against his departure, so he wheeled and rode off.

Crownover, also, went to his mount and stepped up.

Abel grunted to his feet and padded across the campsite. He heaved himself astride, still chewing the twig. "Anything you fellers want us to do?" he asked Dave Beck. The big man shook his head. "*Adiós*, then," Abel said, and reined around with a jerk of his head at Crownover.

As they rode off, Crownover was distinctly conscious of the two tall men standing back there. They were debating his departure in their silent minds, he knew, following the shade-dappled pattern of his back as he and Abel passed along the hillside trail.

There was nothing said until the creek was

reached. From there on they could ride side-by-side. Abel seemed uncomfortable. "They told me about that camp last night," he said, "and asked me to fetch you down there today."

"I don't blame you," Crownover said, but in a tone that didn't actually support the words. "But tell me something . . . why is everyone here so damned suspicious?"

"Well," Abel explained with a blank look, "we got a lot of cattle in here, you see, and right now cattle're bringin' a pretty fair price, and we got to watch out someone don't slip in here and run off a few head."

Crownover looked sardonically at Benton. "Over that trail?" he said, pointing with his chin toward the mountains on their left. "And with a guard up there all the time?"

Abel busied himself with his reins. "It's happened," he retorted. "We've lost a few head out of here, now and then."

"Well, if you have, it was bears or wolves or big cats that got 'em, Abel, not rustlers."

They rode directly to the barn and got down. Sue came across the yard toward them. Crownover took both horses to the corral and turned them in. He leaned on the bars with narrowed eyes fixed dead ahead on the westerly rims. Somewhere out there was a man, and all around him were other men probing the cañons and parks for him.

"Where did you fellows go?"

He turned with a soft sigh to face her. "Up to the Hole."

Abel came out of the barn, brushing himself. He saw Sue and his thoughtful expression creased into a gentle smile. "The trouble with ridin' out," he told her, "is that a feller gets so cussed far from the oven."

She did not smile but searched his face a moment, then said: "Richmond was by an hour or so ago with three of his riders."

"That so? What'd he want?"

"There'll be a herd coming over the pass day after tomorrow. He wants to hold them on the branding grounds here, and he wants you to help cut them."

Crownover was looking at Abel. The older man's face smoothed out, his eyes held to Sue, and a noticeable pause preceded his next words. "Why, sure," he said, with what Crownover thought was excessive casualness, "I'll help." He then crossed to the water trough, dipped in with both hands to sluice off his perspiring face, and flung off the surplus water. "Hot," he said. "Does a feller good to cool off." He threw them both a friendly smile and shuffled houseward.

"What was it?" Sue asked.

"A camp back beyond Brown's Hole against the mountains. Younger, Beck, and Roberts were there."

"Whose camp?"

"They didn't know. They thought I might know."

He saw quick interest, then suspicion, flash across her face. "Did you?"

He smiled. "I got the feeling back there that, if I had, I'd still be there . . . hanging from a tree."

She turned very slowly away from him. "It's . . . never been quite like this before," she said, then looked him squarely in the eye. "I have a feeling, Burt. . . ."

He said—"I had one last night, Sue."—and watched color pour in under her cheeks.

She wavered, on the verge of leaving. Behind

them in the corral horses blew their noses and scuffled dust and made splashing sounds at the trough. A woodpecker drummed with strong persistence on an old pine that sounded hollow. Sue said: "I guess I'd better go start dinner."

"Sue, I thought we were going to talk last night."

"Well . . . that's why I came back. You said good night, remember?"

He straightened, shifting away from the corral fence. "I remember. Maybe this evening after dinner, maybe a little walk. . . ."

"All right, Burt."

As soon as she had passed from view, he entered the barn, got a towel, and headed for the creek through the trees. There, he methodically took a bath and lay for a while where the sun was warmest, then he dressed, smoked a cigarette, and watched the sun dip westward in a flaming arc. When he eventually left the creek, the towel was hanging low on a sage clump, fully spread, to dry.

After supper he and Sue left Abel drowsing on the porch, crossed the clearing before the cabin, and entered the forest. She led the way with sturdy strides as far as a red rock outcropping; there she turned toward him and said: "Pa told me about this morning, Burt. Don't blame him."

His smile was short coming and hard pressed around the mouth. "I don't blame him. I don't blame any of you for being suspicious, really, but I keep remembering something your pa once told me. He said . . . 'You got to watch yourself in Rain Valley.'"

"You've got to watch yourself anywhere, don't you?"

His hard look lingered. "I guess so. But why particularly in here?" He made a sweeping gesture with one upflung arm. "You're a hundred miles from anywhere."

"Not that far," she corrected him, "but pretty far."

"I asked you why, Sue?"

She looked away from him, and in the pale moonlight he noticed that her heart struck sharply against her blouse. "I can't tell you, Burt. I'd like to, but I can't."

"You could put it another way, couldn't you?" She looked up. "You could say you wish you could trust me, but you don't."

"All right," she answered evenly, "suppose I tell you that you're right."

"Have I given you reasons?"

"You have, Burt." She held up a hand when he would have spoken. "While you and Pa were gone today, I rode up the valley trail."

"And . . . ?"

"Burt, you didn't come into Rain Valley in the night because you like to ride in the dark. I think you did it that way because you knew of our sentry."

He stood motionless for a moment longer, then crossed to the red rock, found a ledge, and sat there looking steadily at her, one leg idly swinging, his lips flattened, and his gaze speculative. He had already surmised what she would say next and was thinking beyond that to what he should do about her. "Go on," he prompted.

"Halfway up the trail I found where two riders had come around under the sentinel's knoll. One of the riders cut back into the valley trail, but the second one didn't . . . he went along the rim, westerly, then began dropping down. I didn't follow his tracks. I had to get back home."

He continued to gaze at her and swing his leg. "Can you prove one of them was me?"

She took something from the waistband of her riding skirt and silently offered it to him. It was a horseshoe—one of the shoes he had replaced earlier, before the ride to Brown's Hole. He took it, looked down and up again.

"It's yours. You pulled it this morning. It's too dark now, but you look at it in the daylight, Burt. There's a deep diagonal rock cut across the left bar. I found that same mark west of the main trail where those two riders cut around the sentry's knoll."

He hefted the shoe, then set it carefully aside. She heard him suck back a deep breath and exhale it, then he dropped his head and considered his own idly swinging boot for a moment.

She went closer to him. "Why, Burt?" When he made no reply, she continued. "You knew who made that camp. What is he doing in here?"

His head lifted. "You told Abel?"

"No. I haven't told anyone."

"But you intend to."

"That depends on you. Please, Burt . . . tell me why?"

"It wouldn't do any good to appeal to you . . . to ask you to have faith in me?"

She glanced down at him. Disturbance shadowed her face; her mouth hung heavily parted. "You can't ask that of me. You're here to hurt us. I don't know how, but I know that you are."

In the tumult of her gaze he thought there was also an invitation. He reached forward, touched her with one hand, lightly, let it rest a moment, and, when she made no move away, he put out his other hand and drew her inward and stood up towering above her. His mouth dropped gently to her lips. Her breath shattered against him and triggered something; he bore down harder, bruising her flesh, tightened his hold around her waist, and unexpectedly she let him know she wanted it that way. Her fingers gouged his back and her sudden-flaming desire rushed at him, but in the next moment her hands came up to his chest and pushed at him, pushed insistently until her body writhed against him, fighting clear, and he stepped back. She wavered, put out a hand to the red rock, and balanced there, staring at him from a face made ugly with anger.

"Not . . . like that . . . either," she gasped out. "That . . . you make me want to hit you . . . to hate you!" She put a hand to her lips, rubbed them with the back of it. "You think . . . that will keep me silent? What kind of a man are you, anyway?"

Burt went to the rock at her side and sat down. He was looking straight ahead. "I didn't mean it that way, Sue. I honestly didn't." He looked around at her. "It was the same as last night." He took up the horseshoe and stared at it, then held it out. "Here, show it to Abel if you want to. Show it to Birch Walton."

She ignored the outheld hand and moved farther along the rock away from him, then she paused, leaning there with a hot scald in her eyes. Moments later, after an inner struggle, she spoke in an empty voice. "Why don't you help me believe in you, Burt?"

"Sue, I can't. That's all there is to it."

She turned wearily to face him and said in the same tone: "All right. But let me tell you this . . . you'll never get a single head out of Rain Valley,

Burt. Even if you think you can get around the sentry. Remember me. I know what's in your mind, and, if you try it, I'll warn the others."

He took up his hat, put it on, and stood up. He made a cigarette and held it unlit in his hands with his eyes slitted in an effort to pierce the forest's gloom. Birch Walton as an antagonist faded into insignificance and Sue Benton stood forth twice normal size in Walton's place. He lit the cigarette and exhaled. He had never before been opposed by a woman; it left him hanging in uncertainty.

"We'd better go back," he said, and started off. She followed him through the trees and out onto the fringe of open country, and there she put out a hand and brushed him with her fingers. He stopped, the growing pressure of her hold speaking for her.

"Don't do it, Burt. Please don't."

He saw anguish in her face, in the sharp rising of her blouse, and the parted way her mouth slackened. "I wouldn't dare," he said, patted her hand, and moved off again with his fingers locked hard over hers.

When the cabin was close, he released her. They continued on silently, side-by-side, as far as the porch. Abel's chair was empty and the house was dark.

"Sue? I . . . back there, I didn't mean the kiss the way you thought."

She leaned a little from the porch and whispered: "I can't hate you, Burt. I want to, though. Good night."

He stood briefly after she had gone, looking toward the barn. It took a moment to find the energy to move; he felt drained and tired and old. An owl hooted before he started away. It hooted again as he neared the barn so he cut northerly around the corrals and made directly for the creek. There, his out-spread towel ghostly in damp moonlight, he halted. "I guess you know they found your camp," he said to the darkness.

"Yeah. I watched them. Saw you and the little fat feller come up, too."

"They've got posses of riders guarding every trail. They're making a real hunt of it, Jake."

"I know. But they haven't got *every* trail blocked. I found an old Indian path a couple days ago. It goes right up and over the west rim. It's pretty dim, but it's there all right."

"You're lucky they didn't get you in camp."

The hollow voice laughed quietly. "I wasn't there when they found the camp, but I saw the tracks as soon as I returned, and I moved. Takes a pretty good man to corner me, Burt, you ought to know that."

"You got a new camp?"

"Yep. Right here along this creek, behind Benton's place."

Burt noticeably stiffened. "Hell," he exclaimed, "riders go by here all the time, Jake!"

"I know that. I know just about every rider in this damned valley from a distance. Don't worry."

"All right, but we've got another worry. Benton's girl backtracked us and knows I didn't come in alone. She took one of my horseshoes and compared it with the tracks we made. She even found where you split off."

For an interval the unseen man said nothing, then he made a silent whistle. "What the hell kind of a woman's got that much brains?" he demanded. "She'll pull the trigger on us, Burt . . . or has she al-ready?"

"No. She told me what she knows tonight. Frankly, Jake, I don't know what to do."

There ensued another long silence. "Well, listen," the hidden man finally stated, "that's your end of it. You figure some way to keep her quiet another few days." The voice changed, went lower. "You'd better, Burt. If she talks, you're the one that's out in the open . . . not me."

"I know that," Burt growled. "One more thing. Richmond's bringing a herd in over the mountain, day after tomorrow. They'll cut 'em right here at Benton's meadow."

The formless voice brightened. "Good," it said. "Damned good. Now maybe we can go to work. I think I'd better head back out of the valley tonight, don't you?"

"Or tomorrow."

"Yeah. Anything else?"

"How is your end of it coming?"

"Fine up to now. After they found my camp, though, I guess I'll slack off. Can't very well do what I got to do and hide all the time, too."

"No, I guess not. You think you've got the lay of the valley and the trails?"

"Could draw a map of 'em in my sleep."

"And the other stuff?"

"Plenty."

"Good," Burt said. "I'll meet you here after Richmond's drive comes through."

There came a vague rustling, no more than a sigh in the night, and then Burt was alone. He picked up the towel, shook it free of leaves, and rolled it as he walked back toward the barn.

Chapter Five

Abel told Crownover: "Like as not there are cattle on the south parks, and, if you'd sort of take a look, why then when Richmond's herd comes in, any bolters won't get mixed in with our stock."

This gave Crownover an opportunity to do something he had long wanted to do—explore the valley far south of the Bentons' place. This ignorance of the south country had bothered him a little, but all he said was: "What about Younger and Beck and Roberts . . . won't they do that?"

"They should," Abel agreed, along with a nod. "But let's make real sure. Better safe than sorry, y'-know. It won't take you long. Anyway, nothing much else to do today."

Crownover got his horse, and rode out. He did not cross the front yard for two reasons; he did not want Sue to see him leave and volunteer to ride with him, and he wanted to go out the back way, along the creek, to see if Jake Windsor's camp was visible.

He rode through morning freshness feeling the

rising heat, scaring up birds in the willows along the creek, and once startling a mother mallard with her ducklings. The old bird hit the water with a big squawk and a splash. Behind her came half a dozen lesser splashes, then utter silence.

He did not find Jake Windsor's camp; he didn't even find the tracks he half thought might be in the grass and thickets, which was reassuring, and eventually he came to the roadway, which was crossed as he made for a clearing, and after that he rode now on the road and now in the shelter of timber. By zigzagging he satisfied himself there were no cattle close to the Benton place. It was then noon with a high brassy sun directly overhead and a drowsiness upon the valley. He stopped in the shade, got down, and had a cigarette for the midday meal; he wondered what Sue would think, for by now she knew he was gone. He speculated long on whether she would speak to Abel, and decided she would not. It did not make him feel very high-minded toward himself knowing he was relying on his kisses to keep her silent.

To the south, closer than he had seen them before, Rain Valley's farthermost mountains stood straight up, barren except for pockets of trees, and lower down, little dwindling meadows. For a while he rode toward them, mindful only of seeking with his straining gaze for trails that led southerly out of the valley. He could find nothing except where a dip in the rugged skyline indicated a pass. If there was a way out in that direction, he thought it must be there.

By riding well east of the road, he by-passed Richmond's place, the ranch of Dan Younger, and finally, discernible only by a straight-standing smoke column, the ranch of Ed Roberts. Beyond that, he had no idea who lived this far down the valley.

The black cañon ahead was visible only at intervals until he rode through a thin stand of second-growth trees and came unexpectedly out into a broad, obviously man-made meadow. There was a tinkling creek bisecting this open country, and here he found his first cattle. He was intent on them and for the moment did not resume his study of the pass. Then he struck out over the meadow in plain sight of the dark rock hillsides ahead, which was his last mistake of the day.

Nearing the gentle rise of land where the mountains began, he stopped, seeing that there was, indeed, a dusty trail heading up into the cañon pass. In that second of motionless hush he heard first the flat smash of a rifle up the hill and the space of a sucked-back breath later; he felt a dull explosion inside his head and knew with absolute astonishment that he had been shot.

The jerk of his body made the horse sidestep; he reached for the horn with both hands; a black mist was descending. The horse curved uneasily around, reins swinging. Crownover dug in the gut hooks automatically. Through the roar in his head, he acted instinctively to get back into the trees. There was another shot, but the horse was running now in growing panic, and Crownover continued to hook it through a drowsy nausea. He could not lose consciousness, but neither could he fully direct his actions. He thought in detachment that it wasn't so bad; there was no searing pain as he'd always imagined there must be when a man was shot; there was simply an ache that pounded rhythmically with his heartbeat or, perhaps, with the rising and falling of the horse.

Dimly he thought the assassin would be coming after him to finish it. He did not try to listen for hoof beats. Instead, he waited for the third shot, and this was the hardest thing—waiting to be killed—but his mind was detached even about this. It was functioning as always with a degree of coolness, but as though it belonged to a spectator, not to the man who had been hit.

Tree shadows came up and fell away rearward. The horse was running belly-down. Crownover sensed peril in this wild plunging through forest. He held low to avoid limbs, but it was the slipperiness of matted needles and the abrupt still-standing, big trunks of trees which must eventually knock him off. But it didn't happen like that. The horse, running free, cut more to the east, and came suddenly in his flight to a cutbank tributary creek. He tried to jump, but there was no chance. Crownover felt himself falling—desperate hold broken—then water had him, breaking the fall, cold, sudden, swift-running. He was swept against warm mud, and, there, a delicious benevolence came over him. He felt his body turning soft against the mud, softening out along his spine to where his legs floated weightlessly in an eddying backwash.

When he awakened, there was once more that painful jolting but with a difference now. A constant small vibration jiggled his body and chewed at his mind. Pale moonlight showed strange shadows. He looked out where a pool of water lay and saw the world upside down. He pinched his eyes tightly closed, then sprang them open. The puddle was rearward, the world was righted, and dead ahead was the quick-stepping rump of Abel Benton's buggy horse. He reached up to touch his head and encountered a cool hand. It held his fingers in a moist palm and drew down his head. He did not resist.

"He's heavier'n sin, Daughter. I had to lift him once before."

"Never mind that, just help me."

The last voice was crisp. Crownover felt himself being worked out of the rig and onto the ground, and, strangely, his strong legs held. He looked to his right where two talon-gripping hands held him like steel traps. He smiled. "Sue, you're a mess."

Abel straightened up swiftly, peering. "Boy," he said in awe, "you want to see the last of five hundred, look in a mirror." He inched closer and reached forward a steadying arm. "How do you feel?"

"Headache," Crownover said. "Can I just sit here a minute?"

"A chair, Pa."

"Chair . . . ?"

"Off the porch!"

Crownover's smile dwindled. He did not move until Abel returned and breathlessly pushed the chair under him. "Sue," Crownover said, "any coffee made? I sure feel like I could use a jolt of it."

Sue started past. Abel caught her, said something rapidly under his breath, and let her go. He then worked up a cigarette, lit it, and stuck it in Crownover's lips. The smoke got into his eyes; he closed them.

"Burt?"

"Yeah, Abel."

"You feel up to talkin'?"

"I reckon. Sure could use some coffee, though."

"Sue's fetching it. Burt? Your horse come in all wet 'n' with blood on the saddle. Sue 'n' I backtracked you. Sure Lord, lucky we did, too, you was lying half in the creek. Burt?"

"Yeah."

"It looked like the horse fell with you."

"Fell, hell. . . ."

"Yeah, Sue found your hat. Boy? Who did it?"

"I don't know, Abel. He was a long way off."

"Uhn-huh. You was a long way off yourself."

Crownover removed the cigarette and looked at it, then dropped it and crushed it underfoot. Sue came with the coffee; he drank two cups and felt instantly better. He looked up at her. "Pretty strong coffee," he said, making a dour grin.

"A little brandy, Burt." She sat down. "Did you see who did it?"

"Like I told Abel . . . he was a long way off."

Sue and her father exchanged a glance that did not go unnoticed by Crownover. He leaned back with full consciousness coming in a rush. He felt his head; there was a sticky, matted lump above his right ear. "That feller sure holds to the best spots," he mumbled.

Abel relaxed and let off a sigh. "He holds too high, boy. From a long way off, a man's head's a mighty poor target."

"How do you feel now?" asked Sue, her gaze fully on Crownover's face.

"Better . . . still got the headache, though." He groped for a handkerchief. Sue pressed one into his hand, and he daubed at the wound, then examined the reddened cloth. "Pretty bad, is it?" he asked.

Sue shook her head. "No, it's not very bad. An inch more to the left and it would have been, though."

"Nice neighbors you've got," he told Abel. "I want to meet that one again."

"You were a lot farther south than I expected you'd go, Burt."

He looked around. "What's that mean? What's south of here worth shootin' a man over?"

Abel rubbed his jaw and shrugged. "Well, there's nothin' down there . . . except Birch Walton's place."

"I figured it was Walton," muttered Crownover. "I had a flash it was him about the time the slug hit me." He placed both hands on the chair arms and pushed upright. The throbbing increased in his head from this effort. Sue came up on one side, Abel on the other side; they guided him up to the house, although he could have made it without them.

Inside, Sue got him a third cup of coffee, again laced with liquor. After he drank it, he made a wry smile. "Couple more like that and I'll rush out of here and go cull some wildcats."

Abel's ready smile came up. "Well," he opined, "it could've been worse. Lucky your horse came home. You got any dry clothes up in the loft?"

"I'll get them," Crownover said, and got up. Sue and Abel watched him with concern. At the door he looked back. "I didn't see any cattle south of here until I got to a big meadow . . . that's where . . . whoever he was . . . shot me."

Crownover took his time at the barn. He washed at the trough, let cold water run over the lump above his ear, and as the pain diminished, he considered the possibility of Abel Benton's deliberately sending him out to get shot. It was improbable, he thought, unless Sue had told her father what she knew of him. But even then . . . He shook his head as though it were a fish bowl filled to the brim, went up to the loft, redressed in dry clothing, and came back down to sit in the gloom long enough to smoke a cigarette.

He hadn't seen Birch Walton since the previous Saturday night, but he was reconciled that it was Walton who had tried to kill him. Sue? Yes, it would be over Benton's daughter. Walton had only one other reason and it tied in—the way Crownover had whipped him at the social. He recalled one of the men with Walton saying Birch would try to kill him. He killed the cigarette and got up. A swaying, pale silhouette was crossing the yard toward him. But Birch Walton hadn't impressed him as a bushwhacker—or had he? As Abel said, a man had to be careful in Rain Valley.

"Burt . . . ?"

He moved forward through darkness to stop, facing her.

"Are you all right?"

"I'll make it, Sue."

She brought a water glass from behind her, held it up to him. "Drink this . . . it's for the headache."

He dutifully drank, then made a face. "Lord! What d'you put in that?"

"It's just quinine water and whiskey." She took back the glass and waited. He was looking at her with penetrating attention.

"Have you spoken to Abel about me?" he asked. She shook her head. "I just wondered. Maybe I just rode farther south than I should have."

She straightened, her eyes widening. "You don't think Pa would deliberately . . . do *that* . . . do you?"

He shifted position, stood hip-shot, watching the night light soften and mold her features. "I don't know exactly what to think," he replied. "Anyway, it doesn't matter. Not now. I lived through it . . . and next time it's my turn again." He quirked a strange, cold smile. "First I knocked him down, then he knocked me down, then I knocked him down again, and now this."

"Burt, you don't know that it was Birch."

He ceased to smile. "Who else?"

She had no answer and looked past at the horses moving in the corral. "Come on, I've got supper ready," she softly said, took his hand, and led him slowly toward the house, her fingers holding tightly to his palm, the nails digging a little. Just before they came to the porch, she halted and peered upward. "Be careful tomorrow, Burt. When Richmond brings the cattle down, he'll have riders with him." Her gaze was still and troubled. "Birch will be here. So will the others."

"I'll be careful, Sue. Tell me something . . . do they always work the cattle at your place, here?"

"Yes. They trail a herd over the mountains about twice each summer. . . ." Her voice faded. She turned toward the house, but he held her hand, drawing her back.

"Is this why you wanted me to stay?"

She did not look at him in replying. "Yes. Pa isn't any good at cutting any more. I help, but, well, we never wind up with very good stock."

He examined this in his mind for a moment. "I see. Richmond brings in the cattle and they're split up among the ranchers in here."

"Yes."

"But this is a high valley, Sue, and I haven't seen a haystack in here. What do you do in the winter?"

She half turned as though to point, but it was dark, so she said simply: "That pass you were riding toward when someone shot you . . . that's how they're trailed out in the fall." She looked at him now, but could make nothing of the expression he wore. "Burt, why were you down there?"

"Just riding. Looking around."

"For the southern pass to get out of the valley?"

He could plainly see, even in the gloom, that this thought had been in her mind, affecting her, disturbing her.

"Not particularly, Sue. I was curious is all."

Her next words revealed both apprehension and strain. "You'd never make it. Birch Walton guards that end of the valley."

"Yes," he dryly replied, "he sure does." Then he added a question. "What's he guarding the pass against?"

She pushed up her shoulders and let them fall. "Rustlers . . . strangers . . . troublemakers," she said dully. "It's the way the men are in here. They don't like to be surprised."

Behind them the door slammed and Abel came out onto the porch. He stopped, squinting outward, then he called: "Hey, you two . . . it's time to eat!"

They ate. Abel solicitously and liberally laced Crownover's coffee with whiskey until Crownover would not touch a cup at all. Sue was amused at this byplay.

Crownover was hungry and his mind was busy, too. He made no attempt at conversation, even after he was satiated and leaned back to work up a cigarette. He was considering the aspects of what lay ahead on the morrow. He was sure there would be trouble with Birch Walton. What retained his interest now was reaction among the other men of Rain Valley. Would they, cowboy-like, show only interest in a good fight—a grinning neutrality—or had Birch Walton their esteem? One conclusion he had drawn since meeting the Rain Valley men at Richmond's social was that the cowmen and their suspicions of him would forever be dangling overhead. They would wait, seeking signs that he was a danger to them, and if they became convinced that he was, they would try the same thing Walton had already tried—kill him. But meanwhile, so long as he could walk their knife-edged suspicion without being cut by it, they would respect whatever strength and force he might show, even in a shoot-out with Walton, probably. That, he concluded, was the way cattlemen acted; at least, it was the way other cowmen had acted within his experience and his memory.

He went outside with Abel and sat on the porch. Every muscle and joint of his body was sore, but within his skull nearly all the elfin hammers had stopped pounding.

Abel sighed loudly and made a dolorous head wag. "Youth," he exclaimed in the quiet night, "sure pulls a man through some bad places! Now, if I had that goose-egg on the side of my skull, I'd be down abed. And there you sit like nothin' happened."

Crownover grunted, thrust his legs far out, and stared ahead where moon shadows lay. He did not appear to have heard. "Abel, how many critters did you buy out of this herd Richmond's bringin' over the pass tomorrow?"

"Sixty cows. Why?"

"How many is he bringin' in all together?"

Abel shrugged. " 'Bout two hundred . . . that's the usual number." He swung to look at Crownover. "Why?"

Crownover ignored it the second time. "How many have you bought from him in all?"

"From Richmond . . . oh, maybe three, four hundred head. But that's stretched over the last four years or so."

"Who goes with him to get the cattle?"

"Usually Dan Younger, Birch Walton, a few others . . . but this year he's using just his own crew. Why? What's it matter?"

"Maybe it doesn't matter," Crownover said. "Don't you ever go along?"

Abel made a gesture over his paunch and shook his head. "No. I'm not as young as I once was. Anyway, there's no reason for me to go. They go buy 'em, trail 'em back, we cut 'em here . . . I take my sixty head, and Sue pushes 'em back to Brown's Hole. Only this year, you'll push 'em back for me."

"And in the fall when everyone leaves Rain Valley?"

"Well, I drive 'em, then. I got to . . . they're in front o' me." Abel smiled. He chuckled. "Only way I can get down out o' here is to get the critters out o' here, too. See?" Abel's teeth shone in the darkness. He watched Crownover's profile a moment, then said: "I got another place down south o' here for wintering . . . don't get much snow. Some winters don't get any. But there's lots of ridin' to do and a good snug bunkhouse and plenty good hunting, too." He let it trail off, waiting.

Crownover understood. "I guess it's a good life," he said noncommittally.

Abel pressed forward. "Couldn't be better . . . always hot meals and no rained-on bedrolls. Boy, a feller's got to settle down sometime. It isn't healthful eatin' out of a fry pan all the time. A feller gets worms. Besides. . . ."

Crownover laughed aloud. Abel stopped speaking, and the sound rocketed out into the night around them. "You make a pretty good case for it, Abel. I'll remember you when I'm ready to put down roots."

Sue joined them. The night grew older. Mountaintops cut chunks from the sky, and stars, like congealed, flung-back tears, hung sharply bright across the great curve of heaven. "I brought some goose grease for your head," she said, moving softly behind Crownover's chair, touching him with tender fingers, parting the hair, and laying a cool layer of something sticky against his sensitive wound. He did not stir.

CHAPTER SIX

They were past breakfast and working at catching horses in a leisurely way when Abel drew off with his head cocked. "Listen," he said to Crownover. "They're comin' down."

Crownover had his horse and led him out to be saddled. He shaded his eyes against brightness and looked up the pass. A stone shoulder eclipsed his view but above it hung a telltale banner of lazy dust—light, transparent, drifting, but tan against the azure heavens, tan and soiled. He finished saddling, waited for Abel who also saddled up, then watched Sue fly across the yard toward them from the house. She had on a riding skirt and a white blouse that hurt his eyes to see. Her hair was brushed severely back and held by a ribbon at the back of her neck, and there was fresh color in her cheeks. She flashed him a wide smile, the first genuine smile she had given him in days; there was no trace of poignancy, of pain or doubt or anything—

just the strong will of life. It was a smile he could not have helped returning.

"Which horse?" he asked as she slowed.

"I'll get it, but thanks anyway."

He turned without conscious effort to watch her walk toward the barn. Her waist, small enough, seemed even tinier where a black belt gathered in the folds of that flaring skirt. Lower, where boot tops showed, between the skirt and the tops, each step showed a swish of strong, round legs. Abel interrupted his thoughts from the far side of their mounts.

"She'd rather be astride than anything. Not many girls like that any more."

Crownover returned his attention to the mountainside, and over the small sounds of the yard came a steadier beat of loping horses. He banked away from the rail to watch four horsemen gallop around the house and draw down. The first two, riding stirrup, were Dave Beck and Dan Younger. Behind them, also side-by-side, came Ed Roberts and Birch Walton. Walton's black gaze was quick in searching out Crownover and pinioning him. Walton's free hand dropped a little toward his hip as the others halted.

Beck said: "I think they're comin', Abel."

"Sure, sure," Abel grumbled from between the horses where he was fighting a sweat-stiff latigo.

Dan Younger bent in the saddle with both arms across the horn. "What happened to you?" he asked Crownover.

Before the younger man could speak, Sue came out of the corral with her saddled horse. "There's coffee around front on the porch, if anyone wants it," she said.

Younger switched his attention. He brushed a hand under his moustache and smiled downward, each line of his face showing sincere admiration. "I think the only reason I look forward to these cutting bees," he said slowly, enunciating very audibly, "is because you're along, Sue."

She mounted and threw the dark man a quick smile. Crownover turned his back, swung his horse, and rose up to settle across leather. He did not again look at Birch Walton, but the knowledge stayed with him that Walton was watching him constantly, like one dog watches another dog.

Abel was the last man up, and, with him, it was an effort. When he settled into the saddle, he sighed.

Ed Roberts, reining in beside him, chuckled. "You going to keep tally?" he asked, and Abel nodded as they all knew he would nod.

Dave Beck came up beside Crownover without speaking. They rode forward, watching the people ahead of them until the cutting area was reached, then Beck said: "Quite a lump you got there, Mister Crownover."

"Yeah," Burt replied. "Had my head in the wrong place at the right time."

Beck did not smile; he simply and gravely nodded agreement. Crownover got the impression that Beck knew all about it, and more, too. His face was closed down impassively.

Dimly heard and faint was the lowing of cattle. It was a shifting echo coming off the mountain, first loud, then faint, as Richmond's drive made heavy progress downward. At the cutting ground, unfenced and bare, the grass, long since worn away by hundreds of hoofs, was a large round corral made of immense, notched pine logs. Here, the seven riders halted, swung off, and waited. Easterly lay a narrow run of water and beyond that several hundred yards the forest came down in phalanx formation, sweeping out to a point.

The sun was pleasant and Dave Beck, standing loosely ahead of an angular shadow, made a cigarette and then offered the makings to Crownover, who took them and went to work. "You done much cutting?" Beck asked, folding the paper inward, sticking it with a tongue tip, and firming it up.

"My share, I guess."

"Well," Beck said, and lit up, blowing outward. "We cut an' corral. First, Ed's cut, then Dan's, then mine, then Abel's."

"Walton?"

"Not this time. He bought last fall. He don't want any this trip." Beck considered the smoke in his hand. "Too bad about you two. This isn't a very big valley and trouble has a way of spreading." He looked far up the mountain; the cattle were discernible now, a flowing dark red tide. "Usually before it's over, everyone's taken one side or the other."

"It wasn't my idea," Crownover explained. "I'm just a mite partial to men who manhandle women."

Beck considered this, then looked up. "You mean Sue?"

"Yes."

Beck waited, but Crownover volunteered just that one word. Beck said: "Well, I hadn't heard about that. I thought you just went bronco and jumped him."

Crownover looked out where Younger and Birch Walton were talking. Beyond them, Sue was talking to Abel who had remounted his horse and sat there now with a fat man's sagging discomfort.

Beck, too, turned his head and gazed at the others. After a while he grunted and strolled away. Crownover's face showed vague puzzlement. Dave Beck was a difficult man to assess, but obviously there was something on his mind.

An hour later the first cattle stopped at the creek, running dry muzzles upstream and splashing across from rearward pressure. Powdered with dust, Richmond's riders rode against them with the slack-framed boredom of men long in the saddle, pushing the animals to the very edge of forest where they showed a definite reluctance. Quirts and romals rose and fell; the cattle bawled, then moved hesitantly onward.

Sue crossed to Crownover. "We'd better mount up," she said, but, when he started to turn, she laid a hand on his arm. "Did Dave tell you how we work them?" Crownover nodded, seeing beyond her the way Birch Walton's face had darkened at sight of her hand lying on his arm. "Pa says we shouldn't take any cows over five, Burt." He nodded at her without speaking and would have moved off, but her hand closed down, holding him. "Please . . . no trouble with Birch."

"That's up to him," Crownover stated, knowing in his mind that trouble was inevitable—if not here, then somewhere else, but soon. He withdrew his arm and went to the horses.

Richmond's drive heaved suddenly out of the trees, the foremost cattle stopping still at the sight of mounted men across the clearing and bunching up against the pressure and lowing uneasily. Two horsemen loped around them and crossed the cutting ground. One of them was Richmond, his face cleaner, his clothing less soiled than the faces and attire of his riders. Crownover watched him ride over. He thought Richmond's puffy eyes treacherous, his ruthless mouth bleak and cold, and, although the cowman's face was strong in its structure, Crownover knew a coward when he saw one. He had many times staked his life on his knowledge of men. Richmond was a man who would speak viciously behind a man's back, believing this showed his courage, but he would not speak against a man in that man's presence unless he had a hireling with him to face the consequences. This was, Crownover told himself, a man absolutely devoid of principle, an ignorant man whose entire existence revolved around money and the ways it could be acquired at the expense of others without labor.

Before greeting the others, Richmond called forward: "Who takes first cut?" Ed Roberts kneed forward, and Richmond's adenoidal voice rasped: "All right. Tell Abel how many." He turned then, and rode over by the corral to sit and watch.

As though triggered by Richmond's appearance, the riders fanned out. Crownover took his cue from the others. He rode easterly to complete the large circle of horsemen. In the center of the cutting grounds Ed Roberts and Dan Younger sat still as the cattle poured into the circle. They were uneasy, but only a few tried to bolt. These were turned back handily by the fringe riders.

Roberts worked slowly into the herd, his smile completely erased now. He concentrated on the red backs and began working cows to the edge of the herd. Younger was there. When the animals popped out, he maneuvered to cut off retreat, and Roberts crowded them into a lope, heading for the corral. In this manner he separated thirty cows. When he was finished, there was a moment of respite during which most of the riders smoked, studying the herd.

Abel toted up the tally and called loudly: "Thirty head!"

Birch Walton rode around the corral, opened a gate, and began chousing out the animals. Ed Roberts was there to head them for the south road. He and Walton hurried them, giving no animal a chance to cut back. Crownover and the remaining horsemen kept the balance of the herd occupied so none would bolt in an effort to join Roberts's cut.

The next cut went to Dan Younger. Dave Beck was his partner, and, when forty head had been corralled, Abel sang out the number to Richmond who wrote it down. Beck and Younger then conversed briefly in the center of the cutting ground.

"I'll cut mine in with Dan's!" Beck called out. "We'll separate at his place."

They were moving again when Dan Younger looked at his horse and said something to Beck. They stopped again for a moment before Beck caught Crownover's eye and beckoned him inward. Younger rode ahead to take Crownover's place in the holding circle.

"Dan's ridin' a colt," Beck explained when Crownover stopped in front of him. "He doesn't want to sour him."

Crownover inclined his head and backed off toward the corral as Beck rode into the herd.

Beck was a good cutting man; he and Crownover made a smooth team. They had cut nearly forty animals into the corral when an orry-eyed cow bolted near the gate. Crownover whirled after her. She headed straight for the forest, and Crownover looked up briefly to see who was there to turn her—

it was Birch Walton. He sat motionless until the cow was less than a hundred feet away, then jumped his mount ahead, dipped and swung, blocking her at each shifting pass until she slowed. Walton then swung in hard with a leaded quirt rising and falling. The cow broke back. Crownover had no time to leap aside. She crashed into his mount, head lowered, and kept on going. Crownover's horse landed, stiff-legged but upright. Through the dust Birch Walton was grinning.

Anger flamed in Crownover. It had been a needlessly executed maneuver on Walton's part with only one objective in mind—to dump Crownover's horse.

Dave Beck walked his horse between them and said from an impassive face: "Come on, Crownover, just a couple more and we're finished."

Once, when a critter side-stepped and swung, Crownover was carried by the rush of his horse close to Sue. He saw the tightness of her mouth and the largeness of her eyes as she watched, then the cow was headed and with Dave Beck's help she was corralled.

Abel called out—"Forty head!"—and Richmond wrote it down. There were now eighty cows in the log corral and room for no more. Behind, where the riders were keeping their circle, less than a hundred head remained. Not so crowded now, these remaining animals drifted a little, settling into torpid watchfulness.

Beck dismounted near the corral, flung up a stirrup leather, and loosened his latigo. He then made a cigarette and turned to study the cut. When Crownover rode up and swung down, Beck looked over at him. "Pretty good horse you got," he said. "Any I got would have been dumped sure."

Crownover said nothing. He studied the animals a moment, then turned and leaned upon the corral, looking across where the encircling riders waited, some dismounted, some calling back and forth idly to one another. He made it a point to ignore Birch Walton; there was still anger stirring in his eyes and Beck saw it.

While the horses were resting, Beck said: "We cut Abel's critters and chouse 'em across in his corral." He looked over where Sue sat before continuing. "She usually makes their cut, but I reckon you'll do it this year."

Crownover said—"Yeah."—and flagged an arm at Abel. When the older man came up, Crownover sent him to open the corral gates. He and Beck mounted and sat briefly, still gazing ahead at the cattle. Abel's call to Richmond cut through their separate thoughts.

"Sixty head, Rich!"

Beck punched out his cigarette on the saddle horn and tugged his hat forward. Without looking at Crownover, he said: "Guess I should've said something before. That feller whose camp we found . . ."

Crownover turned. Beck was still looking dead ahead at the cattle to be cut. "Yeah?"

"We found his trail where he came back down into Brown's Hole and crossed it."

"That so," Crownover said, feeling again that inner warning.

"Yes. He was real clever at hidin' tracks, but there's no way to cross the Hole without leaving sign."

"Where did he go?"

Beck finally faced Crownover. "Headed for the creek, crossed it, and came up behind Abel's barn." Beck's steady gaze remained strongly on Crownover a moment, then he lifted his reins. "Guess we'd better make Abel's cut," he murmured, and rode out.

Crownover made a good selection of cows but he did not work them as smoothly as before. There had been in Dave Beck's words and expression a straightforward warning of something ahead. It was this certain knowledge that kept Crownover from fully concentrating on his work.

When the last of Abel's sixty head were corralled, Richmond flagged to a craggy cowboy and the riders closed in, easing the last of the herd, thirty head, down the same road Ed Roberts had taken four hours before.

At Abel's corral, the riders off-saddled. Sue brought coffee, and Birch Walton helped her. Two of Richmond's riders remained with their employer. When Abel thanked Beck for pairing off with Crownover, he offered to send Sue and Burt to help Younger and Beck drive their own cut from the corral to the separate ranches. Beck, thoughtfully subdued, said it would not be necessary, that he and Younger could take care of that, along with their riders.

Richmond stood apart, figuring. When he finished, he called Abel, Beck, and Younger to him. They squatted in the lengthening shadows and talked. Richmond's riders went back for seconds on the coffee, then retired, hunkering near the barn with four other cowboys who had come up near the end of the cut.

Crownover took his horse to the creek, washed its back, then returned to corral it. He was going forward toward Sue and the coffee when Birch Walton drew up in front of him.

"I guess you need a quicker horse," he said in unmistakable challenge. Crownover considered him, then started past without speaking. Sue heard and whitened. The others sensed nothing until Walton raised his voice at Crownover's back. "Maybe it wasn't the horse," he said very audibly. "Maybe it was the rider."

Crownover accepted the cup from Sue, still with his back to Walton. He could see in the girl's face a reflection of other heads coming up, other eyes swinging to bear. He drained the cup and set it down. Behind him, over where Richmond was squatting with the cowmen, there was now total silence. To the north, along the corral where the riders hunkered, not a man moved. Crownover turned. He laid his voice on Birch Walton, strong and definite.

"If that had been an accident," he said, "any kind of a real man would have apologized."

"And if it wasn't an accident?" Walton said in a thickening tone.

"Then the man who did it should have the guts to back it up."

For the space of a withheld breath Birch Walton continued in his slouching stance, then he began very slowly to straighten, his face muddying with color and his eyes widening to encompass everything around Crownover—to see each small movement.

Into this charged and sudden stillness came Dave Beck's voice, thin and softly dangerous. "Sue, get away from here."

Sue did not move and Abel scrambled up, shuffling his feet in agitation but making no prompt move forward. Richmond and Dan Younger also got stiffly upright, but it was Dave Beck who went forward saying: "Hold it, Birch." He went around behind Crownover, caught Sue by the arm, and pulled. She resisted, and Beck said: "Girl, come on."

When she was struggling hardest, Crownover spoke aside, without for an instant looking away from Walton. "Do like he says. Go on."

She went, but twisting free of Beck's grip and going only as far as where Abel stood, slightly in front of Dan Younger and Rich Richmond. She had both hands locked across her stomach.

Dave Beck spoke again, this time letting his words fall into the hush with clear emphasis. "You got a chance, Crownover. Get your horse and ride out of the valley."

"And if I don't?"

"He'll kill you."

Crownover, long suspecting something like that, said now: "And if he doesn't, you others will?"

It was Dan Younger who broke in here. "No . . . no murder," he said. "You'd better saddle up, though."

Birch Walton was waiting.

Crownover could easily see the strain deepening in his face, in the growing dryness of his eyes. Crownover took in a big breath and slowly let it out. He went for his gun.

A sharp cry tore from Sue Benton's throat. Before it could be heard, a gun exploded, its echo plunging straight out toward the forest and there it split into double echoes.

Birch Walton's body hung there, his gun out but stopped in its upward swing, his mouth snapping harshly closed. Then he went down in a heap and folded over to lie flat.

No one moved. Dan Younger looked blankly at the dead man. Abel braced against his daughter's sudden wilting and enclosed her with his arms, holding her up. Dave Beck turned ponderously to regard Burt Crownover. He looked disbelieving. By the corral a cowboy uttered one lone curse, a mild one, and got to his feet.

Crownover let the gun hang, making no move to raise it or holster it, either. He looked at them all from a bitter face. "I guess I stay," he said, then concentrated on Beck and Dan Younger. "As for your suspicions . . . you got a right to them, I guess, and I got a right to call you for them, too."

Richmond's ferret-eyes behind the spectacles were shifting constantly, probing, assessing, seeking for a way to profit from this scene. It was in his mind, although no one then suspected it, that if either Beck or Younger were killed, since their places bordered his, he could enlarge. It was not a substantial thought in his mind, but it was there nevertheless, a predatory thought that could, if conditions warranted, be molded and shaped and acted upon.

"You're callin' us?" asked Dan Younger, his face white in contrast to the black eyes and black moustache.

Crownover was slow to reply. "Only if you want it that way," he said, leaving the challenged men a way out. When neither of them moved after a suitable interval, Crownover holstered his gun. "Abel," he said, "you'd better take Sue to the house."

Abel moved off with his daughter, and the great depth of silence lingered until Beck broke it.

"I can't outdraw you," he told Crownover. "Neither can Dan."

Crownover, with no stomach for forcing a fight, pointed toward Birch Walton. "Then I expect you'd better tie him on a horse and ride on."

The cowboys worked in silence, tying Walton over a saddle, and they all rode heavily from the yard. Crownover walked after them just far enough to see them go toward the corral, pause there a moment in conversation, then run the cattle out and trail after them along the same road Ed Roberts had taken much earlier.

CHAPTER SEVEN

Crownover went to the loft, rolled his belongings, took them down to the yard, caught his horse, and saddled up. As he worked early dusk fell, and with it came a strong, pregnant stillness—something heavily portentous. He finished and straightened up, thinking this apprehension was more in his mind than it was on the land. He pushed his hat back and turned for a long last look over the yard. The quickening gloom blended with his mood; it was bad enough to kill a man any time, but it was infinitely worse to do it this way because now his and Jake Windsor's plans were destroyed. He would have to ride on, at least keep out of sight of Rain Valley's inhabitants, and this was contrary to their strategy. He felt like swearing, but, instead, his jaw clamped closed and his eyes skylined movement from the house. He knew without being able to define the silhouette that it was Sue Benton, and he waited.

She came up to him and stopped, both hands

pressed into the valley between her breasts. Beyond stood the patient horse, saddled and waiting. Crownover's bulky bedroll sat behind the cantle.

"You're ridin' on?" she murmured. He nodded, looking down into her face. She accepted this, moved to the hitch rail, and leaned there, looking north toward the mountains. "You're giving up what you had in mind?"

He let the question pass. "It'd be pretty poor sense to stay here now. Walton was their friend. You can see that, Sue."

She continued to hold her face toward the rising moon. "My father says you're a gunman. He says he never saw a man so fast with a gun."

"No," Crownover drawled. "I'm no gunman. The thing is, Walton wasn't fast. I know your father thought he was . . . but he wasn't. There's a difference," he explained, "between men who spend their lives in the hills and men who live in the trail towns. Hill riders are fast only among their own kind."

"And you, Burt?"

"Well, I've managed to stay alive in the towns."

She was silent briefly, then she said: "Burt, it was my fault, really."

"Your fault, Sue?"

"Yes. If I had told them what I knew, it wouldn't have happened."

"Probably not," he replied dryly. "It would've been me, instead of Walton."

She turned on him. "At least all this . . . other . . . wouldn't be happening."

He saw the frustration, the bitter wrath in her face. "I hate to see hardness in a woman, Sue. It makes them ugly."

"Hardness is reality, and right now I'm trying to

be realistic. I knew you came here to make trouble for us. I told you that."

He untied the horse, ran the reins through his fingers, watching her, seeing the gust of sadness come over her, the mingling of strong emotions. "Good night," he said, and stepped across the horse, shortening the reins. "It would've happened sooner or later anyway. You know that . . . should've known it the first day I saw you." He kneed the horse a little.

From the ground blur Sue said: "Burt? Will you come back?"

"Do you want me to?"

"Yes, I want you to."

"Then I'll be back."

He rode north with a cold containment, already thinking of what must be done and starting out by deceiving Sue Benton. He meant to head west actually, but, as long as she watched, he went north.

An hour later, deep in the forest, he unrolled his blankets and bedded down. When he awakened, the first sun was brightening the tops of trees, painting them pink, then red, with a bold and flashing stroke, but lower, on the mountainsides, it was still gray and shadowy. Around his camp the forest lay thickly, an almost solid mat of spiny branches trapping a nearly pearly-colored light that gradually brightened. The movement of his horse, hobbled and hopping in search of browse, was entirely muffled by the spongy, fragrant surface covering of pine needles. Crownover sought a watercourse, found one, and leisurely washed. He was hungry, too, but that could wait. When he broke camp, he rode westward, knowing without being sure that sooner or later a clearing or an outfall would show him Brown's Hole. He also knew that the Rain Valley riders would know by this time that he was gone. He thought it likely that they had returned to Abel's place, probably late the night before, with their guns, their resolute faces, and a hang rope.

Once he crossed a cattle trail, and for a moment this held his attention. He was a considerable distance west of the Rain Valley trail so this other path could not be a regular route into Rain Valley or even to Brown's Hole. He followed it a mile and came, first, to a snow-water creek and beyond that, a short distance, an opening in the forest that terminated at a sharply inclining hill. There, the path zigzagged downward to a saltlick. Here the scent of cattle was strong, although he saw no animals. Here, also, he found fresh, shod horse tracks and a white mound of recently dumped rock salt.

Crownover left the trail a short half mile beyond the salt ground, tracing out a rugged lift of stony ground. By this time the sun was well above the eastern mountains and a comfortable warmth was in the air.

It was churchly quiet among the trees. His rein chains tinkled, and occasionally his horse tongued the cricket of Crownover's half-breed bit. Beyond these sounds there was total silence.

Where the land turned gently downward, Crownover reined back, riding in a northerly direction until the trees parted, casting him into open country with sunlight quickening everything to light beyond his location, and there he saw Brown's Hole. He had come upon it somewhere below the trail Abel had led him over. He dismounted, took the horse back through shadows into the trees, and fastened him there. Returning then to the clearing, he squatted within the final tree fringe so that he was effectively camouflaged by dark background, made a cigarette, and smoked. Sooner or later, he was positive, he would see riders in the Hole. What interested him now was who they would be.

It was a long wait for Crownover. The sun was nearly overhead before he heard hoof falls behind and above him. Drawing back a little, he watched the upper trail and speculated. He remembered that trail as being very faint. Of course, he was confident every Rain Valley rider knew of it, but the more direct trail into the Hole was over the more southerly and better trail. He wondered if the oncoming rider would be Abel, who had last ridden that same trail in Crownover's company. He waited, listening to the softly walking horse as he had often in his lifetime listened to other oncoming horses in other places—with interest and curiosity, but without fear. Then the rider came through tree shadow and emerged into bright sunlight. Crownover saw him instantly, but without immediate recognition. Not until the cowboy was nearly even with him did he place him—it was one of Richmond's men. He was riding on a loose rein with his head swinging from side to side and downward. Crownover smiled. The horseman was seeking him, or, at least, tracks that would indicate where Crownover had been. He stood up, keeping the rider in sight, but straining to hear other riding men. This man, riding that faint trail, meant Rain Valley's cowmen had established a brush-beating posse to comb the land for Crownover. He went back where his horse was tied and stood with a hand on the beast's nostrils. It proved an unnecessary precaution; the horse neither heard nor scented the cowboy's mount.

Crownover gauged the cowboy's forward progress.

He studied the sun and estimated that, if the brush beaters had started simultaneously, riding from the cutting ground west, they should be about evenly paced from north to south. His best chance to escape them would be to wait until there was a reasonable certainty that they had all gone past, then return to the valley proper. This is what he did. By leading his horse east again and staying to the darkest tangle of forest where there was neither trail to go by nor flinty soil underfoot to echo the passage of his mount's shod hoofs, Crownover made it all the way back to the valley's floor by two o'clock.

He was at the base of the Rain Valley trail. Ahead, unseen but clearly audible, was the creek. Here he mounted, reined north, and prodded the horse upward until he cut the trail. For a time he considered using it but ultimately decided against this, anticipating that the cowmen had not overlooked the chance that he would seek to leave the valley this way. It was a sound precaution—a mile farther up the mountain he smelled tobacco smoke, and a hundred yards farther along he heard a man cough and expectorate. He dismounted, palmed his handgun, and crept forward through a juniper thicket. Less than a half mile above, on up the trail, was Sentinel Butte. There, too, would be another watcher.

The rider had his back to Crownover. He was sitting, relaxed in bright warmth, with a carbine across his legs, his hat tilted forward, and his lips containing a burnt-down stub of a brown-paper cigarette.

"Steady," Crownover said quietly, and followed his echo into plain sight. The cowboy moved only his head. From under a soiled hat brim, two narrowed eyes found Crownover and fixed themselves upon him. Smoke from the cigarette eddied under the hat brim and curled outward. That was the only movement.

Crownover kept a spiraling rock upthrust between him and Sentinel Butte. "Get up," he said, and, when the rider had obeyed, Crownover flagged with his gun. "Now walk over here like you want to get out of the sun. Make it natural."

Again the cowboy complied, and, when he, too, was hidden from view of the overhead sentry, he grounded his carbine and spat out the cigarette, waiting, his face twisted into an expression of speculative interest.

"Let go the carbine. Fine. Now the shell belt."

The cowboy was disarmed, his expression remaining the same. "You better know what you're doin'," he said.

Crownover made a small smile. "I sure better," he agreed. "Your friends are waitin' for me down in Brown's Hole. How many more are up here?"

"Just me," the cowboy said.

Crownover's smile widened. "And the feller on top up there."

The rider shrugged. "And him, yeah."

Crownover holstered his weapon. "How long they been looking for me?"

"Since last night."

"With a rope?"

The cowboy nodded. "What'd you expect . . . you shot Walton."

"You were there," Crownover said. "It was a fair fight."

The cowboy scowled but said nothing. After an interval of silence he flicked his gaze past Crownover and back again. "I work for Richmond.

He pays good. When he says let's ride, I saddle up and ride."

"You've got a real convenient conscience, mister. Lynch a man when you know he hasn't bush-whacked anyone."

The rider's scowl deepened. He shifted his weight and continued to watch Crownover from beneath his hat brim. "I thought about it," he said gruffly. "It didn't exactly sit right with me."

Crownover went to the edge of the upthrust and peered beyond. "Who is up there?" he asked, not caring who the sentinel was, but wanting to be sure he was alone.

"Tom Evans . . . one of Younger's men."

"Anyone with him?"

"No, there's never but one of us at a time up there."

"Will he come down if you call him?"

The cowboy shook his head. "Not allowed to," he said.

Crownover studied the terrain. He and Jake Windsor had skirted the butte nearly two weeks earlier, and it had been no great feat on horseback, but it was a long walk on foot, and Crownover, a lifetime horseman, walked only when he had to. He followed out the way he and Jake had come and sighed. "All right, let's get going," he said. "You walk ahead. Stay west of the butte and keep the trees between you and your friend up there."

It took nearly an hour to get beneath Sentinel Butte. There were slender shadows spreading oil-like from the far side of the trees by then, and the man overhead on watch was in plain view, staring steadily northward where the land fell outward in a miles-long drop off to the great plains beyond. He seemed rigid to Crownover, who was below and behind him, rigid *and* tense. Crownover nudged his companion. "Call him," he said.

"Hey, Tom!"

The sentry started and swung quickly, one hand dipping hipward.

"Steady," Crownover said, the solitary large eye of his handgun fixed on the sentinel's middle. "Move that hand, mister." The guard obeyed with a fiery glare at Richmond's rider. "Go up there," Crownover said to the man beside him, "and disarm him. The first wrong move'll be the last one for both of you." He waited motionless while the cowboy went up the sloping rock, got behind the sentry, and threw his weapons down. Then Crownover went forward to the pinnacle. "Quite a view," he said, turning a brief glance beyond. Then, seeing the piece of polished steel in the sentinel's shirt pocket, he said: "What were you going to do with that?"

The sentinel jutted his chin northward. "There's riders coming down there," he said.

Crownover motioned the two men well in front of him, then squatted behind them, gazing far out. "I don't see anyone," he said. "Where?"

"Yonder . . . see that dust northeast on the flats?"

Crownover saw it, and holstered his weapon with a grunt. He made a cigarette and smoked a moment in silence, watching the steady progress of the riding band far ahead, beyond, and below the mountain pass. "And you were going to signal to Rain Valley about them," he said.

The sentry twisted around. "That's my job, Mister Crownover."

"Care for a smoke?"

"Don't use 'em."

"How about you?" Crownover asked the first rider, holding out the makings.

"Don't mind if I do. Thanks."

The man named Evans was openly uneasy. He said: "What you goin' to do with us, Crownover?"

"Nothing. Unless you get foolish."

The other cowboy lit up and exhaled. He composed himself by sitting cross-legged, gazing out over the valley beyond Crownover. There was a sharp and thoughtful look in his gaze, and, when he spoke, his voice was controlled. "Mister Crownover, a man does what he's got to do to make a living. I reckon that fits all of us. I figure my time is up at workin' in Rain Valley. You got any big objection to me fetchin' my horse and ridin' north?"

Crownover almost smiled. "If you rode north and kept on riding, maybe I would have," he answered. "But a man who'd lynch another man simply because a feller like Richmond says he should . . . I wouldn't put too much faith in that man's intentions any time."

The cowboy was not disturbed by this. He simply nodded his head in acceptance, in simple understanding, and spoke again. "Well, maybe you don't have the big whip hand like you think, though. Maybe we can make a trade, an' I can still ride on." His grave eyes went to Crownover's face and stayed there. "How long you figure it's going to take them riders down there to get up here, Mister Crownover?"

"Two hours if they ride hard. Three if they don't."

"That's about like I figure it. It'll be dark then, Mister Crownover."

"That's all right."

"Mebbe. Mebbe not. You know them riders, don't you?"

"I think I do, yes."

"Well," the cowboy went on, "Mister Crownover . . . in another couple of hours it'll be too late for them to help you."

"Why?"

Evans shot the Richmond rider a sharp look. "Shut up," he ordered.

"It's too late for shutting up, Evans," the cowboy retorted. "Haven't you figured out yet who them riders down there are and who Crownover is?"

"You better shut your big mouth, Bryan!" Evans angrily exclaimed. "Richmond hears about this and you won't be able to ride far enough to ever get clear of him."

Crownover said: "Go on, feller." He shot a hard look at Evans. "Keep quiet, you."

Richmond's cowboy exhaled and looked out where the sun was fast falling. "See, it works like this Mister Crownover . . . a new sentry comes up here at sunset. He'll be along in about an hour from now. Maybe even a little less'n an hour. He'll come armed and, even if we aren't armed now, it'll still be three to one, and, anyway, he'll see the three of us sittin' up here long before he gets here . . . if he ain't already on his way and hasn't already seen us." The cowboy pushed out his cigarette. "Is that worth lettin' me ride on . . . that information that's likely to keep you from gettin' a slug in the back?"

It was worth it, Crownover conceded in his mind, but he feared the cowboy would not ride north. His horse was back down the trail; it would be very simple for him to go down into the valley and warn the cowmen. "I can't let you go," he told the cowboy.

"Not now, anyway, but as soon as we leave here and go back to your horse, you can light out."

"Then," Bryan said, "we'd better start movin', because that relief man's goin' to be comin' up here any time now."

Crownover herded them down off the butte and through growing shadows to where he had left his horse. There, also, he found the other two horses with Bryan's help and took them all into the trees west of the main trail. "Sit down," he told the valley men, then squatted behind them. After a time Bryan said he could use another smoke. Crownover did not offer his tobacco sack and papers; he preferred not having the sentinel's relief locate them by tobacco smoke.

Beyond the forest Crownover was conscious of the mountains—their colors changing toward evening under piling clouds and a breadth of loneliness and silence.

He thought of the oncoming horsemen, and he also thought of Sue Benton. When there was only waiting to be done, especially at dusk, a man's mind wandered. He recalled with particular vividness Sue's anger, her suspicion, and her kisses. They blended in Crownover now to make a small pain. He had felt that identical sensation only once before in his lifetime—a long time ago. When he had been fourteen, there had been a girl with soft blue eyes, honey-colored hair, and freckles over the saddle of her nose; she had been thirteen to his fourteen. Four months after her fourteenth birthday, she had died of cholera. Every now and then in some forest's solitude or in camp upon the plains, Crownover remembered—and the pain came back.

Bryan broke into his reflections. "Rider coming,"

he said, and nodded toward the south. The other valley rider glowered at Bryan but did not speak. He stiffened, though, when Crownover's pistol barrel dug into his back.

"Not a sound," Crownover warned.

The rider was easily discernible as he came steadily on, reins flapping, body loose and unsuspecting in the saddle. Crownover waited until he was abreast, then leaned forward to say something to Bryan.

The cowboy raised his head and called out: "Hey, Clint! Over here."

For just a moment the rider drew upright and shortened his reins, then he said: "That you, Stub?"

"Yeah, it's me. Me 'n' Tom Evans. Come on over. I got something to show you."

The rider drew off, heading for the trees. "Not Crownover?" he said. "Don't tell me you got Crownover."

Bryan did not speak again, and the new arrival pushed his horse beyond the trees to stop dead still. Bryan chuckled at his expression of astonishment. "Naw," he said, "we ain't got Crownover . . . he's got us."

From behind his gun Crownover told the cowboy to get down and drop his gun. When this was done, the rider flashed Bryan a harsh look and spat out a curse.

Bryan's sardonic smile did not wilt. He got up, brushed pine needles from his trousers, and twisted toward Crownover. "All right?" he asked.

"Go on. Just leave the guns where they are."

Bryan went to his horse, sprang up, and reined out of the trees. He cast a final backward glance at the pale and wrathful captives, then struck the Rain

Valley trail northbound. For a long time they heard his mount's shod hoofs over rocks, then the sound faded as Richmond's man passed around Sentinel Butte and began the long-sweeping northerly drop off down toward the great plains beyond.

"Who do you work for?" Crownover asked the captive who had taken Bryan's place.

"Dan Younger . . . and, by golly, when he finds you up here, you'll wish you'd never come to this valley!"

Evans growled. "Sit down, Clint. There's a whole passel of horsemen comin' up the pass on the far side."

The man called Clint threw a swift glance at Evans. "I didn't see no signal," he said.

"'Course you didn't," Evans mumbled. "I never got to send it." He jerked his head toward Crownover. "He got me from behind . . . with Stub Bryan's help."

Clint Ewell considered this, then craned his neck, looking at Crownover's darkening silhouette. "What the hell?" he exclaimed, perplexity muddying his expression. "What's going on?"

Crownover ignored the question, kicked the guns farther back, and put up his own weapons. "When did you leave Younger?" he asked.

"Hour or so ago. Him and the others was working south toward the lower pass."

"They thought I went out that way?"

Clint Ewell said: "Yeah. We covered all the rest of the valley . . . and Brown's Hole, too." He scowled. "Tell me something, Crownover, that other feller who was camped in the Hole . . . you knew him?"

"I knew him."

"Well, just what the devil were you two up to?"

Crownover did not reply, and, beside Ewell, Tom Evans growled: "Save your breath, Clint, he's got the gun, we ain't."

Ewell thought this over. "All I got to say," he told Crownover, "is that, if I was in your boots, I'll be hanged if I'd waste time capturin' folks within a hundred miles of Rain Valley, mister. They'll find you, and, when they do. . . ." Ewell made a slashing motion across his gullet, then he settled back and became silent.

Darkness was fully down and the moon had not yet risen when Crownover heard someone coming afoot, above and north of where he waited. Both Evans and Ewell sat bolt upright, expressions hopeful, and bodies tensed to spring. Crownover drew his gun and moved back where darkness covered him.

"Burt?"

Crownover's muscles turned loose; he stepped forward, putting up the gun. "Over here, Jake."

The oncoming man stopped short, peering downward where the Rain Valley men sat. He waited a moment, then swung his head, gun out and moving.

Crownover went closer. "Couple of the boys from down below," he explained.

Jake Windsor grunted and his expression turned lighter. "How come you're up here? I come on ahead to take care of the sentry . . . an' you got him."

"Gunfight," Crownover said shortly. "I killed their man Walton, and had to ride for it. Came up here, figuring the sentinel'd see you fellers if you came across in daylight."

"Did he?"

"Yes, but he didn't get a chance to signal, so it's all right."

Windsor dropped to his haunches. He was a thin,

angular man with nervous motions and eyes that were never still. "What'll we do with 'em?" he asked, nodding toward the glum and silent prisoners.

"Take 'em along, Jake. What else can we do?"

Windsor got up thoughtfully. "I guess we got to," he opined, without sounding at all pleased. "Where's your horse?"

"Back in the trees with their horses."

"All right. I'll go back and bring the others on. We'll meet you on the trail."

Crownover looked down into the valley where darkness lay. Windsor left, stumbling back up the hill, pushing branches aside. When he could no longer be heard, Crownover went to the prisoners, put them astride, made no attempt to tie either man's arms or legs, but put the lariat from each saddle around his captives' necks, kept the Turk's-head end of the ropes in his right hand, mounted, and in this fashion herded the Rain Valley men down the trail ahead of him.

CHAPTER EIGHT

Crownover waited at the foot of the trail, back in the forest well above the creek crossing. He could follow out the careful descent of the men with Windsor by their hoof scuff and the after-echo in the darkness. Beyond a straight-standing pinnacle against the sky, shafts of quickening light showed where the moon was rising. Along the creek, dimly seen, was a rising, miasmic haze coming off the water. One of his prisoners coughed and spat. Crownover considered them; he felt nothing for either of them one way or the other. He knew how it was—a man took another man's money in wages, and with his labor went his loyalties. It was the elemental simplicity of Western men that was the root of all range wars, all the ceaseless strife. Crownover understood this because he, too, took money for his loyalty, but with him there was also a principle involved.

Jake Windsor came ahead of the dust scent and drew up. "D'you think they'll know we're here?" he asked.

Crownover shook his head. Farther up the trail he had wondered about that and had decided the Rain Valley men would not know. Even if they had returned from their southerly search, they would be at their homes now. They could have seen nothing, heard nothing, and they thought the sentry was up there on the butte.

"I doubt it, Jake."

"Then let's head for the Hole and make camp."

That, too, had occurred to Crownover. He held the lariat tie ends, saying: "Go on ahead, Jake. Take these boys with you. I'll be along a little later."

Windsor accepted the ropes and put an interested stare on Crownover. "You know, if she says anything, Burt, that it'll spoil things, don't you?"

"She didn't tell them before, Jake."

Windsor's gaze went to the creek and across it out beyond the direction of the Benton place. "Her pa might."

"If he doesn't know, what can he tell?"

The other men were looming behind them. Windsor continued thoughtful. "One more night won't make any difference," he said.

"Jake, I want her to get out. Take her pa and go for a ride tomorrow."

Windsor's expression remained unaltered. "I don't like it, Burt. One word now and the cat's out of the bag."

Crownover picked up his reins with unmistakable intent. "I'll bring them back with me, then," he said, and saw Windsor's expression soften with relief. "See you in a little while."

He drew off the trail, watching Windsor's riders trail slowly past on the Brown's Hole pathway. There were eleven of them, and in the tree-night

gloom they looked more than capable. They looked
rough and hard and willing—a gun-wise cow crew
if he ever saw one. After the last man was gone, a
bending wrist turned the horse down into the creek
and out the other side. Moonlight, shades paler and
brighter than before, mottled the land ahead. He
went in a skirting arc where the trees encircled
Abel's yard and halted finally behind the barn, left
the horse, and retraced his steps as far as the north
edge of the house. There, he faintly heard their
voices on the porch, slow and idle-sounding.

"I don't know, honey." There was a pause, then: "I
tried to tell you . . . it isn't in some men to hold still
for long. 'Specially fast gunmen."

"He said you were mistaken."

Abel had his answer ready, and Crownover had to
see the logic. "He's alive an' Birch is dead. A man's
likely to say anything, honey, but you got to judge
'em by their actions."

Sue did not speak again, and Crownover, blending with darkness, wondered how long it would be
before Abel went into the house. He was never to
find out. A horseman walked his mount into the
moonlight near the porch and halted. For a time no
one spoke, then the rider said: " 'Evenin', folks."

Crownover recognized the crisp tones of Dave
Beck and flattened back instantly, thinking Beck had
probably not come alone, thinking also that Beck's
presence could mean but one thing—the cowmen,
perhaps basing their present actions on his known
feelings toward Sue Benton, had come to establish
an ambush. He whirled away and started back to his
horse. If there were others, and he did not doubt it,
they, too, would be arriving, and indubitably one of
them would find the saddled beast hidden between

barn and creek. It had been as Jake Windsor had privately thought, a foolish move on Crownover's part, returning to the Benton place.

The horse was drowsing. It turned a lethargic gaze on Crownover and stirred when he untied it, led it deeper into underbrush, and stepped aboard. South and a little west came sounds of movement through brush farther down the creek. Crownover did not wait; he rode carefully north, paralleling the creek as far as the ford, and there cut westerly until he found the Brown's Hole trace. It took him until the moon was nearly straight up to begin the long-spending descent into Brown's Hole and he was challenged where the trail was narrowest by two carbine-carrying men he had never seen before and one of them took him on down to the fireless camp of Windsor's crowd. There, the sentry left him and turned back. Dark shapes arose off the ground to stand silently watchful as Crownover dismounted, set the hobbles in total silence, off-saddled, and dumped his tack where other rigs lay, and waited until Jake came forward.

Windsor looked past Crownover with his eyebrows climbing. "Where are they?" he asked, apprehension turning his voice thin.

"I didn't get there, Jake. There's an ambush set up."

Jake nodded. "That's no surprise," he said, and looked at the dark man shapes around them faintly illuminated by moonlight. "This is Burt Crownover," he said. "My pardner . . . the feller I told you about." He considered a more appropriate introduction, then shrugged. "Too dark, and, anyway we're all too tired for handshakes." He faced Crownover again. "You hungry?"

"Like a bear cub."

"Come on, we got some tinned beef and hardtack."

Crownover filled up, sitting cross-legged. Around him and farther back were the night-lumpy shapes of men, the swish of sentries' feet passing in the grass, and the low, blurred rumble of voices.

Jake made a cigarette, leaned on one elbow, and regarded Crownover. "I guess you were hungry," he said. "Smoke?"

"I got some, Jake."

The murmur of voices faded. Somewhere close by, a grazing horse blew its nose and stamped. Jake waited until Crownover had lit up. "Had quite a time gettin' up over that old Indian trail out of the valley," he said idly. "Wore my legs off up to the hips." He smiled and moonlight showed off white teeth. "Funny thing was . . . when I was on the rim, I could see those men down there easy as sin, and there wasn't a one of 'em ridin' in the right direction."

Crownover said nothing as he smoked, and Jake studied him, still half smiling. Something tickled Windsor. Something that pleased him to the marrow. It had nothing to do with the hundreds of fine fat cattle around them in the Hole and it had even less to do with what they were shortly going to undertake. When it could no longer be repressed, Windsor said slyly: " 'I knew a girl in Abilene . . . she was tall and she was lean' . . . ever hear that song, Burt? 'She was cross-eyed an' she was mean, the dangedest female I ever seen . . . that Shelley girl in Abilene.' " Windsor put out his cigarette. "Want to hear the rest of it?"

Crownover's sturdy gaze was fixed unsmilingly upon Windsor. "You sure have a strange sense of humor," he said.

"It's just a song, Burt."

"Sure. Just a song. You're about to bust a blood vessel, aren't you?"

"Me? Why, what would I do that for?"

"Over Sue Benton and me . . . that's what for."

Windsor's sly look lengthened. "Well," he drawled, "I keep thinkin' back down the years to all those times when you said a man in our business has got no right to get hitched double with a woman. I keep rememberin' when I married Anna how you stood there by the preacher, holdin' the ring like it was a porcupine, your face as black as a thundercloud."

Crownover tossed his hat aside, stretched out on the grass, and said: "Oh, shut up. You remind me of a magpie. Go to sleep."

"All right," Windsor said agreeably, but making no move to lie back. "But tell me . . . I never got close enough for a real good look . . . is she pretty?"

"She's pretty."

"I saw she was right well put up, even from a distance!" Windsor exclaimed. "But can she cook? You know that's important, Burt."

"She can cook. Now will you shut up?"

Again Windsor agreed in a wholly lazy voice. "Yep, Lord knows I'm tired enough. Just one more question . . . not about her, either . . . about the cowmen."

"What is it?"

"The other day from the rim I counted twenty-one riders. That's nearly two-to-one odds in their favor. What do you think of sending a couple of the fellers south to stampede some horses or set a shed afire or something to draw them down that way before we try to string out the cattle up the pass?"

Crownover examined the idea with his head cradled upon his arms, staring straight up at the sky. "It would slow 'em," he said, "but not enough, and besides, they'd get to the pass about the same time our men did . . . maybe even before, because they know the country better . . . so we'd lose two men and still have the odds against us."

Windsor threw himself back full length. "I guess you're right," he said after a while. "Maybe if we start the roundup at first light, we can hit the trail while they're eatin' breakfast . . . all unsuspecting."

Maybe, Crownover thought, and maybe not. It might have worked that way before he had stirred the valley men up by killing Birch Walton. Now he considered it likely they would not get far up the trail before Beck and Roberts and Younger and Richmond, and their riders, came boiling up the pass after them. He closed his eyes. Sometimes the things a man necessarily did, and felt fully justified in doing, turned out to be his greatest mistakes. Still, he had never for a moment thought the cattle could be taken out of the valley without a fight.

He slept, but only briefly, and, when next his eyes opened, there was silence and stillness all around him. He lay there, wondering what time it was. It must, he thought, be getting on toward dawn. There was a light chill to the air and a scent of dampness. Overhead, hard stars sparkled; lower, the bulk of mountains swelled, silver-soft, against a purple-fading sky. Far up the northernmost peak, ghostlike, seemingly detached from the stone of its nest, between the blackness of the crevice and the blackness of the night, was a solitary small snow field.

He kept looking, wide awake with a gray jumble of churning thoughts running confusedly, without beginning or ending, through his mind, seeing the things around him with hard clarity, feeling again the recurrent slight pain that accompanied memory. Later, although not very much later, a soft glisten came to the sky, the mountainsides turned very slowly to a smoky-gray color, and, as he watched, this became a diluted pink so pale it was scarcely noticeable. Crownover sat up, spat, ran a hand through his hair, and dragged it down over his face. There was a scratchy sound. He reached for his hat and dumped it on. Faintly across the meadow were sleeping horses. Closer were blanket-wrapped dark humps, and in the middle distance lay a tangle of cast-down saddlery, bridles, doubled blankets, booted carbines with butt-plates catching the first thin and watery brightness of false dawn. It was all an ancient pattern to him, a part of life stretching back as far as he could remember. He got upright and moved toward the saddles, found his bridle, and cat-footed it over damp grass toward the horses. A man came out of the tree shadows and watched him. He had a carbine lying across one arm. When Crownover bridled up and knelt to remove the hobbles, the sentinel came closer and grounded his weapon.

"Gets cold in these mountains," he said, "along toward sunup."

Crownover stood up, dangling the hobbles. "Yeah. If you want to eat, I'll watch the horses."

The man nodded, slung the carbine across his arm, and went campward. Crownover had a cigarette for breakfast; as famished as he had been the night before, he was not hungry now at all. He saddled up leisurely, hearing behind him the grunts, the growls, the groans of wakening men. He led his horse out a ways from camp and sighted cattle, some coming up off the ground to graze, others already up, scenting man odor in the dawn and shaking their heads warningly, uneasily, over this intrusion. They would bawl, he knew. There was no way to keep cattle from lowing when you rounded them up, particularly if they had young calves. When they headed them up the pass beyond the creek crossing, they'd protest loudest. There was nothing to be done about that.

He went back to camp. The men whose faces he had not seen in the night were plainly visible now in this new and spreading summer light. They looked exactly as he had thought they would look—hard, capable faces. Not unkind or cruel, but uncompromising and flint-like. Faces of men who would fight or laugh at the drop of a hat. Well, they would be useless if they were any other kind of men. He went on, hearing the quietness of voices, feeling in himself no real desire to speak loudly against dawn's stillness, its silence, and halted where Jake Windsor was saddling up.

Jake cast him a little nod and a slow smile. He knew Crownover had not slept much. "Got any changes to make in the plan?" Jake asked over his shoulder.

"I don't think so," answered Crownover. "Like we agreed before, we split up in the valley . . . have a point man ride ahead up the trail, have four or five outriders on the sides, and the rest of us will stay back in the drag where the trouble will be."

Windsor lowered his stirrup, pushed the latigo's tag end through the catcher, gave it a final jerk, and faced around. "A bad place," he said thoughtfully, "is where we've got to turn them up the trail and away from the valley."

Crownover made no immediate answer. He searched his mind, giving full attention to what lay ahead, before he said: "None of it's going to be easy, Jake, and we'll have to move fast once we start bunching them. They're going to bawl, and as still as it is the noise will carry a long way."

Windsor looked upward at the forest. "But not like out on the plains," he said. "You ready?"

"Yeah."

"Take a couple of the boys and circle them from the west. I'll put the others in place."

Crownover mounted. For a second he and Jake Windsor exchanged a glance, then Crownover reined away. The waiting men were sitting astride, some speaking, some silent, some smoking, and some not—all loose in the saddle and ready.

Crownover made a large sweep with his two men. They did not drive the cattle; they simply rode close enough to encourage the animals to move northerly and easterly away from them. Across the valley, small in Crownover's sight, other riders were doing the same thing. In the background, mountains were swiftly brightening, paling down as far as the meadow where vague light ran out in a warming way over dew-laden turf.

The cattle drifted steadily at first with very little noise, not yet certain they were being driven. A crumpled-horn old cow, trail-wise and calfless, struck upward beyond the meadow, found the trail, and started fully along it. Others followed, stringing out at first, casting glances behind to see that they were not alone. Crownover sent one of his men on

ahead to cut the trail well beyond the crumpled-
horn cow and ride point. He drew back, sitting easily, watching Windsor and the other riders bringing
up the older cows and critters with calves, and finally there was a growing sound of lowing as the
bunched cattle became separated from calves and
voiced distress.

When Windsor swung up, Crownover said: "Jake,
bring 'em on. I'll take some men and ride for the
creek to turn 'em north on up the trail there."

Windsor was frowning. "All right," he called
above the noise, "but what in hell are we goin' to do
with those two prisoners? I can't leave a couple of
men to guard 'em after we hit the pass. We're going
to need all our men with the cattle."

Crownover had forgotten the valley men. He
made a swift decision. "Tie 'em to a tree and take
their horses with us. By the time they get loose it
won't matter."

Windsor's scowl faded. He waved a hand as
Crownover loped ahead, flagging for several of the
outriders to follow him.

Passing swiftly through the forest in a rush,
Crownover led his riders under the trail for half a
mile, then out upon the pathway far ahead of the
herd. Here, the lowing was less distinct. They loped
onward until the creek was in sight. There
Crownover slowed and finally halted. Beyond, under new daylight, the trail toward Benton's range
was visible.

"If we're hit before the herd starts up into the
pass," he told the men with him, "it'll be here. Keep
your eyes open." He spun away, rode on down to
the edge of trees, and halted. Beyond was the Benton cabin. There was a weak rope of smoke begin-

ning to rise above the chimney. As he watched, it grew stronger, spreading out in the quiet air and hanging above the house. He lingered a long moment, then rode back to the waiting men. There was by this time an overtone of very faint sound in the forest. Crownover made a cigarette. Several of the men watered their mounts at the creek.

A younger man stopped beside Crownover and craned his neck up the mountainside. "Good thing that's a rough trail," he said. "If anyone comes after us, they'll have a time of it, tryin' to get past and make us stop."

Crownover looked at the rider from eyes narrowed behind tobacco smoke. "They'll try, though," he replied. "You can bet on that."

"How many head you reckon is in that herd?"

Crownover said—"Five hundred, anyway."—and cocked his head to listen. The lowing sound, muted though it was in the forest, came distinctly now. He twisted for a backward look. The other men, too, were becoming anxious.

One of them said: "I never heard o' such a business as this before, and that's a fact."

In the east there lay a bright band of sunlight where dawn shadows melted before the immensity of a fresh new sun. In among the trees cathedraled light brightened gloom with yellow bands and reflections flared outward from the creek. There was as yet no dust to shatter the prisms with floating mica, but through the vaulted ceiling of pine branches came a quickening in the air, a ripple of reverberation, and growing click of horns, of hoofs grinding in the dust, of lowing cows, and, infrequently, the calls and curses of riders. It was for Crownover an agonizing time, and he had not his first misgivings, but certainly his strongest ones. It seemed ages before the crumpled-horn old lead cow came into view, swinging along in the van, and behind her the pacing tide of red-brown backs. Crownover motioned the riders clear of the trail, placed them so the cows would go up, not beyond, the Rain Valley trail. He was relying heavily on the lead cow to establish the precedent driven cattle relied upon for their course, and she did not fail him.

Dust rose thickly in the air. Unmistakably the sounds were now being made by driven cattle. When Jake Windsor come up with the drag, Crownover sent some of the men on up the mountain to ride on the herds' flanks as outriders, then he wheeled toward the creek, splashed across it—and came face to face with Sue Benton on her sorrel mare, her face showing both apprehension and anger. She crowded her mare near him with an expression turning gray.

"Burt . . . !"

"Go on back," he said to her, and saw the strong reserve of her temper rise against him.

"You said you wouldn't do this!"

"I said no such thing, Sue. Now go on back."

She stared at him, lips parted and ajar, eyes almost black, then she swung her horse, kicked it out into a canter, and the last Crownover saw of her, she was sitting in ease on the running animal slightly swaying. She did not stop at the house but passed on, riding hard, down the valley over the southern roadway.

Crownover turned and went swiftly up the trail after the last rider, pinching his eyelids down against the dust, the sunlight, and the bitter thoughts in his mind.

Small calves hung back and worried mothers gave full tongue to their anxiety. Jake Windsor twisted to watch Crownover come up. He was swinging a plaited romal at the reluctant calves, the last man up the trail. "I guess she heard!" he called out.

Crownover threw him a look. "By now everybody in the valley has heard," he growled.

Dust thick enough to chew was lead-like in the air; it had a sweaty, salty scent, and the farther up the mountain the drive went the stronger it became. Crownover, riding behind Jake Windsor, turned for a downward look at the first wide bend. There was a hurtling, thin vapor of dust coming up the valley, visible over treetops. He halted to watch an opening, to await what he knew would soon show—riders.

When they came in full sight around the last finger of forest, thundering toward the Benton place and beyond, to the lifting thrust of upward trail, Jake Windsor also saw them.

"She did a real good job," he rumbled, speaking of Sue. "But maybe we're far enough up." He swung back and stopped beside Crownover. "I think we can keep 'em rifle distance away."

Watching the horsemen speed steadily through the trees, hit the creek in a flying spray, and wheel in a press of men and animals to the right and start on up the trail, Crownover told Windsor: "You'd better send someone on up the trail and tell those outriders not to let any of them get around us."

Jake rode off, and Crownover, feeling perfectly relaxed, waited for the valley men to pop out of the final fringe of forest, coming strongly on uphill. When they did, he had no trouble at all in identifying the first two riders—Dave Beck and Dan Younger. Crownover got down, unshipped his carbine, and let off two quick shots, both close. Beck set up his horse in a flinging slide, and Dan Younger, struck from behind by another horseman, shot on ahead another twenty feet before he could stop. A pistol shot came into the echo of Crownover's gunfire. The distance was too great; Crownover remounted, and reined on up the trail.

He met Windsor with four men hastening back in response to the shooting. "Never mind," Crownover said. "Just keep pushing 'em until we're over the summit. Jake, stay here with me. We can keep them from getting any closer."

Windsor drew forth his carbine with a fluid motion and squinted down where the valley men were milling, guns sparkling in the morning brightness, horses excited and sweat-darkened now. "Must be every man-jack in the valley down there," he said. "Looks like maybe twenty of 'em."

Crownover said: "Take a good look at that rider to the left of the big feller with the black moustache."

"I see him . . . the little feller," Jake said. "What about him?"

"It's not a *him*, Jake. That's Sue Benton."

Windsor puckered his eyes. "What the hell is a woman doin' with 'em?"

"That's no mystery," Crownover replied. "Just don't shoot any more."

Windsor held briefly silent. When he spoke again, he laid the full weight of his scorning judgment on the valley men. "Bringing a woman along to hide behind," he snarled. "I guess they're no better'n we thought they were."

"No, Jake. They didn't bring her. She just came to see me caught. And don't think Younger there or that other tall one . . . Beck . . . are cowards, because they aren't."

Behind them the lowing cattle faded on up the pass. Riders' shouts, the clatter of hoofs over shale rock, the eye-stinging dust, all retreated toward the summit beyond where Crownover and Jake Windsor sat. Farther down the mountain horsemen mingled, spoke sharply amongst themselves, casting bitter, bleak stares up where the two mounted men sat, carbines ready.

Windsor's thick jaw, whisker-stubbled and weather-stained, hung slackly. "They aren't even going to rush us," he said finally, his tone thickening with disgust.

"They're trying to make Sue go back," Crownover told him. Then: "Look farther down. Those two riders coming up."

"Who are they?"

"One's her father, Abel Benton. He can make her go back. I think we'd better get ready to go on after the herd."

"Who's the other one?"

"That's Rich Richmond, our man. Keep an eye on him, but don't worry, he won't take a shot at you because he's too damned yellow to get within gunshot distance of someone who might fire back."

Windsor's attention reverted to the first little fat man. "You're right," he said swiftly. "He's making her go back."

Crownover waited only long enough to see Sue turn her horse, begin the descent, then he said— "Come on, it's too exposed here."—and led the way up the trail in a bounding run.

The trail fell off steeply to the east. There was no

danger from that direction. But to the north where talus and granite sloped gradually upward and away, it was possible to ride a horse with no great danger, and Crownover thought Younger and Beck would bring on their crews by bending around the trail, over the westerning rises, and come down upon the cattle somewhere near the summit. He explained this to Windsor when they slowed finally near the drag riders, and Windsor craned to see how much farther it was to the leveling off of the trail's climb. He shook his head. "They can't make it in time, Burt. The lead critters are already over." He made a quick grin. "I think we held 'em off long enough."

"Long enough for what?"

"To get out of these cussed hills. That's all we want, isn't it?"

Crownover, conceding this, made no reply.

CHAPTER NINE

Crownover saw the point rider top out, hesitate on the skyline, and begin the descent down the far side of the Rain Valley trail. He thought grimly they had had better luck than he had expected, and left Jake to ride part way up the westerly side hill, pick his way through junipers, buckbrush, and manzanita until he could see back down into the valley and down the rearward trail. There were seven riders walking their horses up the path. They seemed grimly intent on slow progress. For a moment this puzzled Crownover. The riders were making no attempt to catch up; they were simply blocking off the trail behind them. It came to Crownover that this was exactly what they had been detailed to do—cut off retreat back down into Rain Valley.

He urged his mount another hundred yards west, and sought movement. It was not difficult to locate. Sweeping upward now, after skirting the side of the far hill toward the summit, were the balance of the valley men. Leading them were Dan Younger and

Dave Beck, carbines in hand now and faces set unalterably for the top.

Behind Crownover the drag was making its slow progress upward. Crownover saw at once the valley men would intercept it. He got down, went forward as far as the windwarped trunk of a squatty juniper tree, and dumped a solitary shot in front of Beck. The big man drew up quickly with his head swinging. Seeing no one but hearing easily the drag's bawling calves, he called something back to the others, and they immediately began fanning out, heading for tree, rock, and brush cover. Crownover did not risk a second shot; it would have given his location away. He went back, mounted, and jogged stiffly over the rock field to its final drop off to the trail below. There, he called to Windsor and the men with him in drag position.

"They're behind me, fanned out, and coming over the hill!"

Windsor left one man to push laggard animals and brought forward the other drag riders to stop near Crownover.

"This is a bad place," he panted. "Can we hold 'em?"

"We can turn 'em back," Crownover said sharply. "We've got to." Far below to the north, morning sunlight lay across the plains farther than a man could see even at this elevation. "We've got to make them head for the plains and try for a stampede."

Windsor dismounted and went forward, leading his mount. He was the only man visible at first. A carbine exploded in the thin air. Rock flew upward in front of him. He went flat and pumped off two wild shots.

The valley men, encouraged by Windsor's fall,

sprang forward. At that moment Crownover and the others ran over the crest and fired a sudden, ragged volley. The valley men retreated in alarm, and Crownover saw Richmond's rotund shape waddle away with greater speed than he would have thought the small man capable of. He called to Windsor and sprang astride to push the advantage. It was a good maneuver; the valley men raced back to their horses in a hail of slugs, mounted, and spun away over their own back trail.

Crownover reined up, watched briefly, then turned back.

Jake Windsor was dabbing at his cheek with a soiled handkerchief. "Flyin' rock," he said, and swore. "First blood."

Crownover solemnly removed his hat, parted his hair, and showed them an angry red gouge in the scalp. "That was first blood," he said. "Couple days ago."

They continued on along the ridge, skirted Sentinel Butte, cast a slow, searching glance backward, then, seeing no pursuit, began the descent.

For an hour there were no more attacks. Windsor was worried. He waited well behind the others, looking upward. Not long afterward he saw seven men top out and halt in a group, gazing downward. He called to Crownover, pointing to them. Crownover recognized them as the rear guard of valley men. They caused him no concern. What was troubling his mind now was where Beck and Younger had taken the others. They had not given up, he knew that, and yet there was no sight or sound of them. He rode back where Windsor was again pursuing his downward course, and reined in close.

"When you were scouting the rims," he asked, "did you find any other trails except this one and the old Indian pathway?"

Windsor wagged his head. "No," he said, "just those two. But that doesn't mean there aren't others. I only had a few days to look around, you know."

Crownover considered—the mountains west of Sentinel Butte were sharp-spired, steep, and gloss rock stone. Still, a man like Dave Beck, or Dan Younger for that matter, knew every inch of these hills. Even if it would normally be perilous to attempt skirting around the mountains horseback, with a thousand foot fall on the off side, Beck and Younger would know the safest place to try it, and they certainly had motive enough. He lay a long, troubled gaze on the distant leveling off of trail into prairie.

"If they get around us, Jake," he said slowly, "we've got to keep them from stampeding the herd back into the mountains. We don't want to lose them now."

Ahead, dipping rumps awkwardly swinging from side to side, heads low to the trail, and dark hides glossy with sweat, cattle were strung out nearly a downhill mile. Their dust lay heavily on outriders, men watching each open place in the trail more than the animals around them, guns riding easily across thighs or balanced upright.

Behind them, Sentinel Butte stood craggily sparkling in the sunlight. Beyond it was nothing but sky. It was no longer possible to see Rain Valley at all, and the north slope, with fewer trees but more huge boulders, made it impracticable for the valley men to attack here as long as Crownover's outriders kept vigil, which they did, quartering the land ahead in big sweeps. They could have tried it, Crownover thought, and with their numbers they might have gotten a man or two, but they could not have approached the trail or the fortress boulders without first crossing a naked shale slope and they, too, would have lost men. He gave Beck and Younger more credit than to attempt this; they would know where to strike and they would be waiting.

It seemed to Crownover strange, this riding ponderously downward in the warming light of new day, hearing cattle bawl, seeing riders moving leisurely, waiting with a dry throat for an attack that would certainly come.

Jake Windsor returned from a short scout and pushed back his hat, made a cigarette, lit it, and blew outward. "Mile more, maybe," he said. "Possibly a little more'n that."

"Listen, Jake, the girl might be with them again."

"You saw her go back, Burt."

"Yeah," retorted Crownover in a voice gone as dry as cornhusks, "I saw her go back. But I know Sue Benton, too. When she hates, she hates all over. Abel won't be able to make her keep out of it." And, thinking of their kisses, Crownover added in a different tone: "Maybe she's got more right than any of the others, too."

"Some of the cattle hers?" Jake asked, mildly interested.

"No. It's not that."

Windsor understood. "Oh," he said, and continued to smoke, his nervous, alert eyes constantly probing the land ahead, the boulders nearer the trail, and the flung-down, golden gauntlet of prairie beyond the mountains. "Well, don't worry, pardner,

the boys know the difference 'tween a ridin' skirt
and a full blouse from pants and a butternut work
shirt," he said.

Little snakeheads of dun dust burst from beneath
their horses' hoofs. The setting was temporarily
peaceful and Jake Windsor studied Burt Crownover
from the edge of narrowed eyes. Crownover had always possessed a self-confidence that had never
failed to draw Jake's admiration. They had been together in some bad spots these last few years, and
never once had he seen Crownover shaken off his
feet. He seemed never to forget their mutual inter-
ests and to remain constantly alert to their common
goal. There he now sat, rocking along with a poker
expression, without fear—and yet with something
unlikely in his eyes, something close to pain. Windsor should have felt sympathy. They were close
enough, had been partners a long time, at least as
time was figured in their trade. Crownover had
"stood up" for Jake at Windsor's wedding down in
Laramie; he had nursed him through a bad lung
wound once; he had always been there, rock-like.
But Jake felt, instead of sympathy, amusement.
Crownover, the rugged stalwart who had turned
aside dance-hall girls after months away from the
sound and scent of women, had been skewered
straight through his soft parts by a slip of a girl with
red-gold hair and a two-edged temper. It was funny.
Jake did not smile, but irony lay in his eyes. He recalled something his wife had once said of
Crownover: "You wait, Jake, when that man finds
the right girl, he'll change so swiftly you'll think
he's a different person."

Well, the change was there. So far only Jake had
seen it, but Jake wasn't the only friend Burt

Crownover had. The others would also see it—if they got these dog-goned red-backs out of the mountains all in one piece. Jake thought now the others would react the same way, too. They would be gravely solemn and impassive outwardly, but inwardly they would be watching with masculine amusement the crumbling of big Burt Crownover's iron-like outer shell.

Jake put out his cigarette and dropped it. He made a big sigh and tilted his head to see down where the point rider was angling closer to the prairie. "Won't be long," he said. "Where do you reckon our Rain Valley friends are by now?"

Crownover lifted a heavy arm, pointing northeasterly. "There," he said. "Somewhere."

They were beginning to feel the leveling off; their saddles no longer tilted forward precipitously. Jake considered a moment ahead of speaking. "We'd better pass on around. The drag will follow now. It's all downhill from here to the plain."

They drew off up the side hill with their drag riders and started a stiff-legged trot toward the serpentine head. Outriders closed in as they came abreast and responded to Crownover's forward-flung arm by trailing after in their wake. Near the juncture of mountain flank and plain was a final, long screening of dark pine trees. Here, where the rising heat of the prairie met the mountain cattle with a furnace breath, the animals tended to pause, to wander into shade and coolness. Here, too, the balance of Crownover's riders was having trouble forcing animals out onto the treeless, heat-writhing prairie.

Burt gave Jake an order and spurred on ahead. It would be here, Crownover thought, that the Rain Valley men would make their strong attempt to turn

the herd back. Nor was he wrong. His mount had
scarcely left the trees when a flat, echoless carbine
shot sprang out of the reach of trees from the west.
Crownover, expecting attack from the east, whirled
in that direction, running hard for cover. A second
and third shot went after him, then the thin, high
cry of a man somewhere back with the cattle—a cry
of acknowledged and recognized peril.

Crownover hit the ground ahead of his horse and
ducked into tree shadows. Behind him, startled cattle, fully exposed out on the plain, stood, stiff-
legged, sensing danger. They stood thus for only a
moment, then they ran. Red backs, rattling horns,
lolling tongues, and crashing hoofs striking with
the voice of panic upon the level, dry ground. Stampede, the terror of every range man, accomplished
what Windsor and the men back in the trees had
been fruitlessly endeavoring. It hurtled the drive out
onto the prairie in a welling tide of cattle. From his
hiding place Crownover came upright from a fighting crouch to watch.

The animals, trail-tired and hunting relief from
lowland heat only moments before, now went
wildly forward in a maddened, senseless rush. They
fanned out over the plain in a hurtling red froth of
dust, glistening hides, and panic. Crownover
stepped across his saddle, swung in and out among
the trees as far as the point of juncture between trail
and plain, and over the roar of nearly 500 blindly
running animals shouted at Jake and the others.

"Follow them! Use them for a shield! Get out of
the trees!"

The men did not understand Crownover's words,
but they understood his swinging arm and his

wheeling example. They burst past the last trees, riding low and hard in the towering dust of their stampeding herd. There were gunshots from the west, but there was little to fear. In the confusion, the speed, and the dust, no man presented much of a target.

For a mile Crownover, who had done an insane thing, had deliberately worked his frightened horse through the stampede from east to west, made no attempt to turn the leaders. He could not have turned them anyway, until their panic had passed. He rode, twisted upright in the saddle, seeking the others. They could not be counted in this shifting, dust-drowned turmoil, but when he saw a man, he gestured him forward. In that way he finally attracted Jake's attention.

Windsor was riding a leggy grulla gelding with an ugly, bulging head, sullen little eyes, and a ewe neck. The horse possessed only one desirable attribute— he was built from poll to crupper, from frog to withers, for running. When Jake caught Crownover's signal, he jumped the grulla out in a spurt of sudden speed and swiftly closed the distance.

Behind them, others, seeing the leaders converging toward the lead cattle, quirted and spurred to come up. Far back, skeletal mountain flanks steadily retreated and the rising dust hung like a backswept banner obliterating in part that deadly last fringe of forest.

Between them, Crownover and Windsor tried repeatedly to bend the lead critters. It could not be done until, three miles out over the prairie, the cattle began to tire, to slacken in their headlong rush. Then the leaders gave way a little, swinging easterly in a great arc, and the oncoming riders, seeing wha was being done, leaned their mounts purposel along the west side of the red wave.

The entire stampede, from its inception to its fina slowing, had not consumed more than forty min utes, but the herd was scattered over an area large than Rain Valley's entire domain. Crownover drew down to a stiff walk and counted horsemen. Ther was not a man missing, but six men were scattere far to the west by the blind rush of cattle. They wer pushing easterly in an angry drive to join with Crownover and Windsor, driving relentlessly the stumbling and exhausted critters.

At Crownover's side Jake spat dust, removed his hat, and dragged a soiled sleeve across his forehead. "Like the man says," he exclaimed to Crownover, "things happen for the best, but, pardner, there sure are times when I doubt it! When those fool critters started to run, I was plumb in front of them. You talked about scairt men . . . pardner, I was two dozen scairt cowboys rolled into one hide."

Crownover settled forward in the saddle. "I didn't see Beck's men," he mused.

Jake swung a brief look mountainward. "Can't expect to see much in that dust," he retorted. "But don't worry, they're back there somewhere."

Across each man's thoughts came then a rollicking cowboy yell. They both turned. The westerly horsemen were sweeping up fast, driving an increasingly large herd ahead of them.

Burt watched a moment before saying: "I can't see where we lost many, Jake."

"Right now that doesn't interest me half as much as getting down on my prayer bones near a creek with shade around it," the shaken Jake Windsor said tartly. "Even your Rain Valley friends don't mean much right this minute." He was profusely perspiring and his lips had not recovered their color yet.

The heat came down with a physical weight that pressed men deeper into their saddles. Ahead, trudging easterly with reddened eyes and slavering mouths, the cattle continued over the prairie scarcely making a sound now. Crownover strove to pierce that immense and soiled dust cloud, and, when this had been accomplished, he studied each man. They seemed only dustier and with sweat-darkening shirt fronts. He detected no limping horses or hangdog men.

For fully half an hour the drive went forward uninterrupted. When it was east far enough to see past the lingering dust bank, Crownover made out shimmering shapes coming along in their wake. He tried to count them and failed, but it was Beck, he knew, and Dan Younger with the Rain Valley men.

It was pointless to try and hurry. Even if the men and horses could stand it, the cattle could not. He took Jake Windsor and dropped back, instructing the riders to keep the herd moving east out over the plain where the horizon faded in dim distance to merge with lower, vaguer mountains in that direction but many, many miles off.

"You think we can hold 'em off?" Jake inquired.

Crownover shook his head, seeking, finding, and strongly watching the oncoming horsemen. "Not out here we can't," he told Jake. "We can slow 'em for a while. But Beck's no fool . . . he'll split the crowd up and send 'em east on both sides of us."

"Damn," said Jake quickly, "what's the sense of letting 'em flank us, Burt?"

"We'll drop back. Don't worry." Crownover calculated distance with narrowed eyes. "Still too far," he said, but pulled out his carbine anyway and rode with it in one big hand, waiting for the Rain Valley men to close up on them. Jake followed his example.

When Burt eventually stopped, Jake also did. Crownover raised his weapon, took long aim, and fired. Here, on this endless, walless, roofless prairie a carbine shot sounded insignificant—a faint cork popping. But the Rain Valley men hesitated, which was enough. Jake employed guesswork elevation when he, too, fired, and luck smiled. A distant horse sprang straight into the air and lit bucking hard. The rider lost his hat, his carbine, and finally both stirrups. He went off rearward with a thin, very faint cry. Jake smiled. "Be damned," he said, and chuckled. Crownover also smiled.

They watched their enemies go to the downed man, help him, remount him on the stung animal, and mill in a small circle, evidently talking.

"They'll try to pass us now," Jake said.

But they didn't. With recognizable big Dave Beck out ahead, they came steadily onward at a swinging walk. Sunlight sparkled from bits, from belt buckles, and from carbines at the ready.

"That's foolish," Crownover growled, raising his gun again. He fired almost simultaneously with Jake that time, and Beck's mount did not jump, it simply collapsed—folded its legs feeling nothing, and going down with a strike that spurted dust upward over the scrambling rider.

"That ought to hold 'em," Jake muttered.

It did. Dan Younger flung down to assist Beck to arise, standing back while the unseated horseman beat dirt from his clothing, each line of Younger's posture screaming silently of uncontainable wrath.

* * *

'or an hour Crownover and Windsor held the Rain
Valley men back. Jake finally asked: "What the dev-
l is wrong with them? Why don't they split off and
:ide down our flanks. Even an Indian's got that
much sense."

"Not when he's as mad as Beck and Younger are,
he hasn't, Jake. They want us right now even more'n
they want their critters back."

The Rain Valley riders made an occasional shot,
but Crownover had a close estimate of the distance
and kept well beyond range. After a time he said:
"Jake, I think that lucky shot of yours made them
cautious. They're acting like they believe you're car-
ryin' a rifle, instead of a carbine."

Jake grimaced through sweat-streaked dust. "I'd
hate to have to duplicate that shot," he answered.
"They'd know soon enough it was a lucky fluke."

Crownover was silent for a long time. The overhead sun was moving slightly off center. He regarded it thoughtfully. "I never thought we'd still be
holding them off in the afternoon."

"That gives me an idea," Jake interposed.

Crownover lowered his carbine. "I know," he responded. "I think I've got the same notion."

"What?"

"They're not pushing this fight after Beck got
dumped for a reason."

"All right . . . but what reason?"

"Nightfall, Jake."

Windsor inclined his head. "Yup . . . it's the same
idea," he conceded. "Just keep us in sight until after
dark, then . . ." Jake made a large circling gesture
and worked his free hand as though it held a pistol.
"In the dark," he concluded. His forehead wrinkled

as he studied the riding party between them and th[e] mountains. "But I thought you said they weren' afraid."

"They're not."

"Then why back off from two-to-one odds?"

"This feller Dave Beck," explained Crownover, "i[s] a cold, reasonable, and practical man. He aims to ge[t] the cattle, but he's not going to risk losing half hi[s] men to do it."

"The patient kind," Windsor drawled, watchin[g] where Dan Younger and Dave Beck rode the sam[e] horse.

"He's patient, Jake. He's also dangerous. I don'[t] think he'd back down from anything."

"You sound like you got to know him, Burt."

"No, I never got to know him, really . . . just sized him up. I'd say of all the Rain Valley men, he's the damnedest. I'd also say, if someone made a fool out of him, I wouldn't want to be the man."

Jake's attention wandered. Behind him, spread out and sluggishly moving ahead under the encouraging cries and curses of the riders, cattle streamed steadily eastward, scuffling dust and lowing hoarsely for water. Jake, wise in the ways of range critters, sniffed and bent a long stare beyond toward the hazy mountains. "We'd better hit the Chugwater pretty quick or those damned things'll sprout wings again." Jake considered a moment, then said with emphasis: "But this time, I'll be behind them."

"They'll stampede again," Crownover said with such conviction that Jake looked quickly at him. "Beck and Younger will try to stampede them right over the top of us in the dark." Crownover looked down. "You didn't think they were simply going to reclaim the cattle, did you?"

CHAPTER TEN

The afternoon wore away. Several times riders came back where Crownover and Jake rode to squint at the distant pursuit and ask questions. Patiently Burt told each man the Rain Valley men were waiting to close in after dusk and that he thought they would attempt to stampede the cattle west again, back toward the pass, and, if possible, over the camp of the Crownover-Windsor crew.

It was an unnatural, almost eerie chase. The Rain Valley men could have overtaken Crownover's crew at any time during the afternoon. Instead, they stayed far back.

As the prairie haze of afternoon settled and the sun reddened where it stood poised over far-away mountain peaks, thirsty cattle bawled incessantly. Jake, too, said something about a drink, and Crownover, who did not have a canteen, either, told him to put a coin in his mouth to keep saliva running.

The first long shadows were spreading downward from the westerly mountains where there came to the cattle a freshening coolness in the air; they quickened their steps instinctively. The saddle horses also found a reserve of new energy to draw upon, and Crownover cast a look back where the Rain Valley men were visible, then said to Windsor: "Chugwater. I think we've made it."

It was another long mile before shadowy willows stood up from the plain and the lead critters began a shambling trot forward, bawling for the water they smelled. No attempt was made to hold them back or even direct their course. The cowboys drew off until Burt and Jake came on, then they fell in around the two.

One of the cowboys, craning to watch their pursuers, said: "Maybe them boys're goin' to get a surprise." Someone chuckled. There was the sound of men booting their carbines, clearing their throats, and speaking in lighter tones back and forth.

Crownover went ahead with the others to water his mount. On either side of him for half a mile were cattle. Most of them had waded right into the water and were standing now, tanked up and lazy, dull-eyed with repleteness. "Camp in the willows," he said to the crew. "Jake, keep a watch, I'm goin' on ahead for a ways."

Beyond the Chugwater River was more prairie, but it was possible now to make out the shapes of the Laramie Mountains beyond the dun flow of plain. Crownover loped steadily onward until moving specks, dead ahead, appeared over the curve of prairie, then he slowed to a walk, and finally, with the oncoming horsemen in view, halted altogether.

The first man up was a graying, fiercely moustached, and hard-eyed individual on a big black horse. He showed recognition when he stopped, but offered no greeting. "You get 'em?" he demanded. Crownover nodded. "Where are they?"

"On the river."

"And the others . . . the fellers you took 'em from?"

"Following, like we thought they'd do."

"How many?"

"About twenty."

The big man grunted. His face relaxed and he crossed both hands over the horn. "Never thought it'd work like that," he rumbled. "All right, Burt, you figured it right. I brought another ten men . . . that ought to make more than enough, hadn't it?" Crownover inclined his head again, and the big man lifted his rein hand. "Then let's go on. It'll be dark directly."

The crowd of horsemen headed for the Chugwater, following Crownover. Thickening dusk mantled them. A mile along they heard bawling cattle. Here, Crownover cocked a look skyward, estimating how long it would be before full darkness.

The big man on the black horse kneed up beside him and said: "There's a pretty bright moon these nights, Burt."

"We'll come up from behind the willows, Henry," Crownover replied, and continued riding until he saw, faint although distinct, the spidery willow shapes and, beyond them, the dull and metallic sheen of last light on water. Here he halted. "They're west of the slough," he said. "I think they'll come slippin' up after dark and try to run the cattle over us and back toward the Rain Valley trail." He paused. "Henry, do all these men know one another?"

"No," the large man answered. "But the ones with me know each other . . . mostly they're neighbors."

"Then I reckon," said Crownover, "that we all ought to tie our handkerchiefs around our necks. When I go ahead, I'll tell the others to do likewise."

Henry Warner understood, and said: "All right . . . anyone 'thout a neck rag will be a Rain Valley man."

"That's it. I think, if you fellers wait back here until it's good and dark, and then move in before the moon comes up, we can get the thing done without a lot of shooting." The big man rumbled agreement, then Crownover spoke again. "One more thing, Henry . . . there's a girl with them."

"What?"

"A girl. Tell your men to be very careful."

"What in the . . . ?"

"She is Sue Benton, daughter of Abel Benton."

Warner digested this with a fierce scowl. "What'd she come along for?"

"It's a long story, Henry. Just tell your boys not to shoot first and look second."

"All right. What you going to do, Burt?"

"Same as you, only we'll make a camp where they can see the fire, then we'll cut out afoot as soon as it's dark and see how the hunting is." Crownover waited a moment, and, when Henry Warner said no more, he touched his hat and loped back toward the Chugwater.

Jake Windsor was waiting. He was chewing jerky and standing toward the west, obviously seeking to distinguish man sounds over cattle sounds, a pointedly useless undertaking with close to five hundred critters bawling and stamping and settling with loud thumps upon the dusty ground.

When Burt stepped down, Jake said: "I got five men scouting to the west." Jake offered a twist of jerky, and Crownover took it. "I sent 'em off afoot, so our friends can't skyline 'em."

Crownover stepped down heavily, as a tired man does. "Start a little cook fire," he said, and, when Jake's expression turned saturnine, Crownover said: "Sure, they'll see it and know it's a ruse, but we've got to have something to sight on before the moon comes up."

As Jake moved to obey, Crownover sought the men. He sent several forward to locate and bring back the scouts Windsor had sent forward. He then returned to the river, flattened there, and sluiced coolness over his face, and also drank. The ground was good; he was tempted to lie there, to let his body loosen powerfully all over. Instead, he got up, flung away excess water, and watched the sky darken while he chewed jerky. He was worrying now about Sue. Perhaps she would stay back— probably would, at least until she thought it was safe to seek him out and burn her anger and her scorn against him. If she didn't, maybe Abel could make her stay clear. He went back thoughtfully where Jake had a little pencil-flame rising up into the gloom, made a cigarette, and smoked it while watching the men approach through the murky, fast-failing daylight.

When they were gathered, he said: "Listen, Warner is out there with the others . . . ten of them. As soon as it's dark enough, we're all going forward on foot. We'll have to work fast, because I think the Rain Valley boys'll want to take advantage of the darkness, too."

Jake stood up, moving well away from the fire-light so he could not be backgrounded by it. "You take half the men and go east," Crownover told him. "I'll take the rest and scout around to the north. They'll be horseback, so you ought to be able to skyline them. You'll be afoot, so they won't be able to distinguish you from the critters." He paused a moment, peering at the trail-grimed faces. "Understand?"

"Yeah," a lanky rider said, "but what do we do with 'em?"

"Take 'em alive. Shoot only if you have to. Just remember this," Crownover said, laying solid emphasis on his final words. "You're afoot . . . if there's a lot of gunfire, those cattle'll stampede again . . . they'll run you down, and there won't be enough left to put in a matchbox."

The riders stirred, shot looks back and forth, and manifested some uneasiness. It was, Crownover saw, a prospect that had not escaped them. One older man squatted down and methodically began creating a cigarette. When it was lit, he said: "Maybe we ought to take our ropes along. Pretty hard to unseat a mounted man from the ground 'thout you rope him."

Crownover said it was a good idea. The men then stood around, eating jerky, going to the river to drink, smoking, and patiently, stolidly, waiting for Crownover to tell them it was dark enough.

Crownover looked at the sky a while. When he could no longer discern the westerly rims, he sent the men for their lariats.

While he waited, Jake made a smoke and considered it skeptically in his fingers. "You know," he drawled thoughtfully, "if this works, it'll be the first time I ever heard of such a scheme comin' off."

"They're out of the valley, Jake. They're on the plains now," Crownover stated. "Whatever can go wrong can't hurt us too much."

Jake shrugged. "The cattle're clear of the hills, anyway," he replied. "I guess that was the main thing."

When the cowboys returned, they split up. Crownover took his crew and started away from the Chugwater. By this time cattle appeared as clumsy shapes against the earth. They avoided them when possible in order to minimize restlessness among the animals, striding westward until they encountered less and less of them. Crownover stopped where an ancient buffalo wallow depressed the ground, and listened. Beyond, out over the plain, there was only night stillness. Behind them came the infrequent lowing of the herd.

"Last I seen 'em," said a cowboy, referring to the Rain Valley men, "they was off to the left there."

Crownover made no comment; he thought it likely that Beck and Younger had split up, too, each taking part of their crew around the herd toward the Chugwater. He started northward over the prairie, and within fifteen minutes he knew he had made a correct guess—there came softly to his hearing a shod hoof striking stone.

Without a word the riders spread out. Two men shook out their ropes. One of them was grinning wide enough for his teeth to show in the darkness. Crownover squatted low, sighting upward. He saw the moving figure by its blurry advance, tracked its oncoming course easily, and motioned for the men nearest him to get ready. The entire sequence of events worked perfectly. Crownover's men knelt to skyline their man, then positioned themselves so that he would pass them close by. Finally the grinning cowboy rose suddenly from the ground as the rider moved past, swung his arm once in a backhand toss, and the rope settled neatly in place. The valley rider made a startled sound in his throat before he left the saddle to land hard on his back. Before he could sit up, there was a handgun four inches from his face, and a tight knot of grinning men crowding closely.

Crownover took the man's gun, threw it outward, and yanked the man to his feet, seeking recognition. "Not a sound," he growled, and the cowboy obeyed. "You're one of Richmond's men, aren't you?"

"Yeah. What the devil d'you fellers think you're doing?"

Crownover made no answer. He faced the roper and made a motion. "Stay with him until we get a few more." To the captive rider he said: "Where are the others?"

"Comin'," the man said, turning sullen.

"Following you?"

"Yeah. But you fellers won't get 'em. Dan Younger's leadin' them an' . . ."

"Shut up," Crownover ordered. "Now sit down," he said, and pushed on the cowboy's shoulder, forcing him down. "Don't open your mouth." He jerked his head, and the other men moved out with him, leaving the disgruntled valley man and his captor behind.

Darkness was settled fully now; it was difficult to see ten feet ahead. Crownover could distinguish his men by their neck-wrapped handkerchiefs, but in this it sometimes took a second look; none of the handkerchiefs were white at all.

A wiry, short man brushed fingers over Crownover's arm. "Comin'," he whispered. "Two of 'em ahead there."

Every man dropped down. Dark shapes came dimly down the night, side-by-side. Crownover's men shook out loops and tensed where they squatted. As before they let the men pass before standing upright to cast, but this time there was a sudden interruption—far to the south came a crashing pistol shot. It startled one roper and he missed, but both horsemen had jerked up suddenly, peering off to their right. Two more ropes sailed upward, then came swiftly down and jerked tight. One of the astonished horsemen let off a sharp cry. The next second he left his saddle and fell atop his companion. One of the men was struggling to reach his belt gun. A scuffed boot came out of nowhere to settle with crushing force upon the cowboy's wrist. He looked upward, twisting his body, then he said through clenched teeth: "All right . . . you don't have to break it." The foot drew away and someone jerked both men to their feet. The two recognized Crownover, the killer of Birch Walton, when he thrust up close.

"How many more are behind you?"

"Three," the uninjured man said quickly. "Dan Younger and two of his boys."

The men were disarmed and sent back to join the first captive. Crownover waited briefly, then headed farther out over the plain, northerly. He wanted Dan Younger particularly. He had nothing against the cowman except that he was a leader. If they could capture both Beck and Younger, the Rain Valley riders would be like sheep.

But he didn't get Younger. He didn't even find him. There was a sudden sharp exchange of gunshots to the south, and closer, dimly discernible in the night, cattle sprang up off the ground to turn, stiff-legged, and face the explosions. Crownover wanted to swear. Fortunately the firing was some distance off.

A burly cowboy, alive to immediate peril, said: "I'd feel better if that was farther east. If them cattle run, they're goin' to come right for us, headin' north." He watched Crownover, waiting for him to speak. He got back no comment.

Crownover was waiting, balancing in his mind a decision to head back for the river or continue onward. When the firing began again, swelled, and rocketed over the shattered stillness, he decided in favor of the river. "Run for it," he said, and set out in a jog parallel to the bedded herd as far as the spot where the captives were standing stiffly erect and nervously watching the cattle.

"Bring them along!" cried Crownover, and hurried on.

They got to the edge of the herd before the gunfire, swelled now to skirmish proportions and moving, from the sound of it, back westerly over the prairie, and there they stopped. Crownover said— "Get to horse!"—and made for his animal.

A breathless man came swiftly out of the night and suddenly halted, seeing the mounting men between him and the willows.

Seeing his uncertainty and sighting the neck rag, Crownover said: "Friends. What's going on over there?"

The rider came swinging onward again. "Big bunch of them Rain Valley fellers," he said rapidly. "I was with Jake's crew when we roped two of 'em, but before we could shut 'em up, they started hollering, and then the others come up."

"Get your horse!" Crownover ordered, then started south in a long lope with his mounted crew behind him.

They skirted the milling, lowing cattle and rode for the gunfire without a pause until there were visible gun flashes, then Crownover tugged up his carbine and stopped.

"Damned dark," someone growled. "You could shoot your own paw in a spot like this."

Crownover silently agreed. It took moments to determine where the separate battle lines were drawn, but, when he had this fixed in mind, he took his riders nearly a mile south, then west in a steady lope until he thought it safe to come down behind the fighters. He made one mistake. He did not consider the possibility that some of the Rain Valley men would retreat. Now, trotting forward, he was suddenly run down by a group of racing nightriders. There was no time to seek neckcloths or even get clear. Two horses collided and went end over end. Someone fired a gun and someone let off a startled, loud curse, then the crew was scattered, fighting their horses out of the way, and Crownover found himself ahead of four men who had no neckerchiefs and whose handguns were swinging to bear. He ducked low and rode hard into the west, straining to increase his lead or get clear. He could do neither. The withdrawing Rain Valley men had horses equal to his, and they were now intent on driving this solitary horseman out over the prairie ahead of them. There were several shots, then a voice roughened by excitement bawled out: "Don't shoot, dammit! You'll bring 'em out here after us." Crownover, with no idea who the shouter was, felt relieved at his words.

Riding hard, he heard the steadily oncoming pursuit behind him. At the end of a twenty-minute run, he twisted to look back. He had increased his lead a little, but the horsemen were still coming and they were clearly bent on riding Crownover down. He had no alternative, and it made him ashamed when he did it, but he roweled his horse hard for its last burst of speed and drew away in the darkness. One pursuer, seeing him dimming out ahead, fired. A second shot came, then no more because he was lost to sight.

Crownover swung north and made excellent progress. He slowed eventually, letting the horse gulp air, and finally, farther along, he halted altogether. For some reason that he could not then fathom, his pursuers had also stopped. He could distantly hear nervous horses snorting, rolling their bits, and stamping, but no actual sounds of additional movement. He went back a short way, listening. There were several ragged parts of spoken sentences, but not enough, nor did Crownover go closer. Instead, he went carefully out and around the horsemen, bound back for the Chugwater.

When he was close enough to see uneasy cattle stirring, nuzzling calves, and occasionally lowing, he became very conscious of the otherwise stillness. No longer did even the echo of gunshots remain. He dismounted while still unable to sight the river and stood motionlessly for moments. Then he went very slowly forward until Jake Windsor's little smoldering campfire was visible. By then a ghostly paleness was coming from beyond the farthest mountains, and, as he walked, it continually brightened until the moon arose, aloof, cold, and silvery, with a lopsided, heeled-over appearance.

"Freeze!" a voice called sharply, and a man rose up off the ground with a cocked handgun held steady. "Who are you?"

Crownover made no answer until the sentry had moved into his sight, then, seeing the man's rumpled handkerchief, he spoke his name. The nighthawk put up his gun.

"All right. The rest of 'em are down by the stream. Couple of 'em went off a while back, lookin' for you. Figured you got the deep six durin' all that shootin'."

Crownover passed on.

CHAPTER ELEVEN

Jake's small guttering fire had been fed until it burned brightly, casting immense and dancing shadows against the willows and the river farther back. Men moved solidly and mostly in silence among horses still saddled. On the ground with arms lashed behind them sat the valley men. They, too, were mostly silent. A short distance off a number of men were in violent dispute. Among them stood Jake Windsor, dwarfed by the huge, thick body of Henry Warner.

Crownover made for this group, leaving his horse in the care of a man who came forward to express surprise and pleasure that Crownover had not been killed as most of them had thought. He was still some distance from the arguing men, when he heard someone exclaim angrily: "Dammit, Henry, you know blamed well we come along just to get hold of these fellers!"

Warner's bull-bass rumbled a hard answer. "No, I don't know any such thing, and, if I had known it, you wouldn't be here now, so put that in your pipe and smoke it!"

Crownover pushed through. Men turned to stare and Jake was momentarily rooted where he stood, then he smiled and that was his only indication of pleasure. "Thought they got you," he said succinctly. "Glad they didn't."

Warner fixed a bitter eye on Crownover. "Where in hell you been, anyway? You know what these men want to do?"

Crownover was looking into faces closely. The men moved back to include him in their circle. In the reddish light he saw their hard eyes and the unfriendly expressions, then Warner was growling again.

"You got up this crazy idea, now you talk some sense into these fellers. They want to string up those valley men."

"That can wait," Crownover said finally. "Where is the girl?"

Henry Warner's fierce expression gradually faded. "I don't know," he said. "There's no girl among the prisoners."

"How about her father . . . Abel Benton?"

Warner shook his head. "We got a list of their names, Burt. No Abel Benton among them."

Crownover turned to Jake. "Get your horse," he ordered. "I ran across four Rain Valley riders, out a ways, heading back toward Rain Valley. She'll have to be with them."

Jake started away, and Henry Warner said— "Wait, I'll go, too."—and pushed out of the crowd. A number of other men also volunteered, but, when Crownover broke away from the willows, he had with him only four men, including Jake Windsor.

Henry Warner was not one of them, and, as Crownover rode off, Warner called out: "Meet us in town! We'll be waitin' for you there!"

The way west and south was illuminated with moonlight. Crownover did not push the horses, realizing that the group he was after could not make good time—they had already used up their mounts this night.

It was on the downside of ten o'clock before the southerly mountain ramparts were close enough to distinguish tree shadow. It was ten-thirty by the time Crownover's riders struck the trail and started swiftly up it. A little later Jake Windsor spurred ahead, got down, and studied the dust for perhaps a hundred feet, and, when the others swept up, he swung back across leather, pointing ahead. "Not more'n ten, fifteen minutes," he said.

"How many?" called Crownover.

"Well, I know you said four, but I make out five sets of tracks."

They made it to the summit before Crownover sent Jake ahead to scout up the trail; he did not think the fleeing Rain Valley men would attempt an ambush, but he wanted to be certain. It proved to be a wise precaution but a useless one; the cowmen got all the way to the creek on the south side of Rain Valley trail without meeting anyone, and there Crownover halted again. This time he told the men to skirt out through the forest and encircle the first set of buildings they came to. Jake understood. After Crownover had kneed his animal on across the creek, he explained to the others the first ranch was the Benton place.

Crownover went forward as far as the final line of trees and halted there, peering outward toward the dark Benton buildings. There was no light, as he had expected. But it was, he thought now, a useless precaution because he could smell dust and horse sweat in this thin night air. They were there all right, probably waiting to catch the first pursuer over a gunsight. He drew out the carbine and stepped off, touched the ground lightly, moving in an angling way to command the front of Abel's log house. He tried to think of some way to get them out into the open so that Sue would be clear of gunfire, but it had been a grueling twenty-four hours—he was not only physically weary to the marrow but he was also mentally drained. He halted finally near the cutting grounds easterly, and leaned upon a giant fir tree.

An owl hooted and the echo rang out of the trees behind the barn. Crownover continued to stare at the darkened house a moment more, then he straightened off the tree and called out.

"Abel, come on out! The place is surrounded an' you won't help matters any by bein' foolish."

Silence. Far back the owl hooted again, a lonely, sad sound in the moonlight.

"Sue? It's all over. Tell them to come out."

That time Crownover got an answer, a bitter, savage response hurled against the night.

"You got the cattle, wasn't that enough . . . you murderer!"

"Sue!" Crownover called. "I'm coming to the house. I want to explain this to you."

The silence returned deeper than before, and Crownover, teetering forward, hesitated in his tracks. Five of them in there, four of them men with guns and reason to kill him.

"Sue," he cried, "tell them to hold off until they've heard me out!"

That time a man's voice came back and it, too, was savage, but with a difference; the man was taunting Crownover. "You said you was comin' forward! Well, come on!"

"You'll hold off?"

The man snarled a fierce laugh. "Sure, we'll hold off . . . until you're clear of the trees." A pause, then: "Are you Crownover?"

"I am. Sue knows who I am."

"We all do," the man said, "and we owe you something. Come on out in the open and collect it, Mister Crownover."

Crownover tried again to catch Sue's attention. He let the silence come down and remain unbroken for a full minute before raising his voice again. "Sue, listen to me! All I want is ten minutes of your time. I'll come up there unarmed."

That time a voice Crownover recognized at once as belonging to Abel Benton came from the house. Abel did not sound angry, he sounded hopeful, and, where he stood, Crownover could visualize the older man's worried countenance. Abel was not a violent man, he knew.

"Mister Crownover, walk out where we can see you and leave your guns back there in the trees."

"I have your word, Abel?" Crownover called.

"You have my word, Mister Crownover. We've talked it over and we can use you as a hostage if we're surrounded. Are you coming?"

Burt put aside the carbine, shucked his shell belt and holstered handgun. "I'm coming out, Abel!"

He stepped forth into the moonlight and began a slow-pacing advance upon the house. He heard a carbine grate over wood and thought it was tracking him, but it was not a reassuring sound and Crownover's throat turned dry. Ahead someone opened the front door, drew it far back on unoiled hinges, and loomed faintly in the dripping darkness of the cabin's interior. There was a black sheen where cold metal caught and held the faintest light, and eighteen inches higher a pale oval.

"That's far enough," a man said, stopping Crownover at the porch's edge. "Tom, see is he plumb unarmed."

Burt recognized Tom Evans at once and felt the cowboy's wrathful stare cut into him. Rough hands beat the length of his body, then Evans said: "It's all right, Al." He gave Crownover a hard shove onto the porch and toward the door.

The inside of Abel's house was blacker by far than the night beyond. Someone came up behind Crownover and pushed him into a chair. He could at first make out only the movement of men in the room and the black shine of guns, then Abel was there, bending closely, peering into Crownover's face.

"How many boys did you fetch here with you?" he asked dispassionately.

Crownover lowered his arms when he replied: "You're completely surrounded if that's what you're wonderin' about, Abel."

"But, Mister Crownover, why? You got our cattle. Why do you want to kill us too?" Abel's expression was full of puzzlement and frank curiosity.

Crownover made no immediate reply. He strained to locate Sue in the darkness. It was impossible, so he spoke her name.

From across the room there came a rustle of movement and a hard-toned: "What do you want?"

"I want to explain this to you," Crownover said, and would have said more, but a man thrust his face up close and snarled at Crownover.

"Yeah, you do that, Crownover. You explain. It's goin' to keep you alive ten minutes longer."

This, too, was a familiar face. The other captives had called this man Clint, and Crownover remembered him. He told the cowboy: "Shut up and listen, mister. And if you think you're goin' to gun me, guess again." There was solid resistance in his words. "Even if you want to, an' I don't really blame you and Evans for feelin' like it, you'd better use your head. The first shot brings more guns again' you than you'll ever live to see a second time. Now back off."

The cowboy's breathing came sharper, but at that moment another looming shape laid a hand across Clint's upper arm and spoke quietly. "Let him have his say." Sue had crossed closer to Crownover's chair.

Behind her, he was beginning to make out the still shapes of men. "We didn't steal those cattle," he told the girl.

"No?" She challenged him bitterly, but Abel put out a hand silencing her.

Abel's gaze was fully on Crownover in a breathless, waiting manner. "Go on," he said softly.

Crownover put up a hand, rummaged in his shirt pocket, and held forth his palm with something silver-like lying across it. Abel and Sue had no trouble seeing it. The girl's indrawn breath sawed into the darkness, and behind her crowding men craned forward. One asked quickly: "What is it?" And Abel made a soft reply. "Marshal's badge, boys."

Crownover dumped the circlet back into his pocket and never once looked away from the girl. "This has been going on a long time, Sue. This rustling cattle from flatland ranchers and bringing them in here." He shot a glance at Abel. "Maybe some of you didn't know you were buying stolen cattle. I hope for your sake you didn't." The long gaze lingered on Abel, but there was nothing to be read in the fat man's face. Crownover continued, returning his gaze to Sue. "That feller who was camped at Brown's Hole . . . his name is Jake Windsor. He's out there now with the others. He's my partner. We rode this country for a month before we figured the only way to get cattle out of here was over the valley trail. We didn't want to try to bring a posse in here. In the first place, it probably would have been seen before it got over the pass, and every man in here would have taken to the mountains. In the second place, if you people were riled, we figured you'd stampede the cattle into the mountains, too, and we'd never get all of them back again."

Abel leaned back and his chair squeaked. He looked upward at the other men and sighed. There was nothing to say.

"So," Crownover went on, "we made it look like we were rustling from you, so you'd follow and try to get the critters back." He paused. "You know the rest. There was another posse waiting out by the Chugwater. They've got every man except the people in this room."

Abel scratched his belly. "Mister Crownover," he said evenly, "did you get Dan Younger and Richmond and Dave Beck?"

"Yes. They're on their way to Laramie right now with the U.S. marshal."

"Henry Warner?"

"Yes . . . Marshal Warner and his posse."

"I knew Warner years back," Abel said in a fading tone.

Crownover gazed at the faces above him. Sue Benton was big-eyed and motionless. The riders were impassive, each face swept clean now. It was Abel who broke the stillness.

"Do you know who stole them critters each year?" he asked Crownover.

"I know who did it this year, Abel. Richmond."

"Mister Crownover, we always bought our cattle from Richmond. Every year."

"How about Beck and Younger?"

"Well, sometimes they went with Richmond, but I don't know whether they knew where he was gettin' the critters or not."

Crownover got up; the scuff of his boots was loud in the room. "All right, I'm your hostage," he told the group of stony faces. "But it won't do you any good. Those men out there aren't going to trade me for you, so the next move is up to you."

Abel got up off his chair. "We'll go back with you," he said. "I tell you honestly, Mister Crownover, there was a time or two when I sort of wondered about them cattle, but I never knew actually that they were rustled."

That, thought Crownover, would be the substance of each man's defense in court—they had wondered about the cattle but they hadn't known they were stolen. He began working over a cigarette. "Tell me something, Abel . . . why did Birch Walton try to kill me?"

"Well, I expect it was over Sue."

Crownover lit up and gently shook his head. "I kind of doubt that. Maybe that was part of it, but it wasn't all of it."

"I'll tell you," a cowboy blurted out. "It was because you was gettin' too close to findin' out how the surplus stock was driven south through the mountains and peddled to the cowmen down south in Colorado."

"And Walton knew what was going on?"

"Sure, he worked hand-in-glove with Richmond."

Crownover looked steadily at the speaker. "But you boys didn't?" he asked.

The men stirred. They looked at one another and at the man who had spoken, who said, carefully choosing his words: "Well, a feller gets paid to ride and he does what he's told. 'Course, now and then he wonders about things."

"Like what?"

"Well, Mister Crownover, before I come up here to ride for Dan Younger, I worked for the Horseshoe Dot outfit north o' here beyond the Dakotas. After I'd been here a little while, I seen Dan and Birch brandin', and, like you probably know, Dan's brand was a wagon wheel." The cowboy looked around briefly before he finished. "All you got to do to make a wagon wheel brand over a horseshoe dot is close the horseshoe circle and put a few spokes emanating outward from the dot."

"So," said Crownover, "you knew they were rustling."

"No, I didn't!" the rider quickly protested. "I wondered about it, sure, but I didn't *know* that was what they was doing."

Sue turned abruptly and went into the kitchen.

Crownover watched her go, and then said: "Abel, how about lighting a lamp?"

As pale light glowed, growing stronger, Crownover looked more closely at the men in the room. Some he recognized, but there were seven of them, not the five he had expected. The additional two men were easily explained; they were the men Jake had left tied at Brown's Hole, and, of the riders, they seemed most contrite now.

Abel alone found it possible to smile. "Sue's makin' some coffee," he said genially to Crownover. "Why don't you fetch those fellers outside up here?"

Crownover went to the door and called. There was no answer, but drifting forward from different positions came Jake Windsor and the others. Behind Crownover there was a solid sound of something heavy being placed upon a table, and Abel's pleasant voice speaking.

"Boys, I expect the best way to keep the peace would be for us all to sort of lay our guns here, on the table."

When Jake trooped up onto the porch with the other men, Crownover motioned them inside. They did not exchange a word, but the disarmed men across the room exchanged dull glances with the newcomers as Crownover crossed to the kitchen, hesitated briefly in the doorway, watching Sue, then crossed to her side.

"I'm sorry," he said.

"You could have told me, Burt."

He stood a full minute with his thoughts taking him back, feeling the reproach in her tone. "I know that now, Sue. I didn't know it then."

"You thought Abel knew about the cattle."

It was distasteful to him the way this conversation

was going; he didn't want to remember the past weeks at all except that night down in front of the barn and the other night, out in the forest where the red rock was. "I couldn't be sure about anyone in Rain Valley, Sue, and I had my life on the line." He knew without looking down that she was facing him, but he felt her presence strongly against him. "The thing that was tearing me apart inside was what you would think."

"I understand, Burt. I didn't mean the things I said. All the way back here I wanted to die because I thought you were a rustler and I didn't care. I wanted you and I knew I'd go to you. I'd find you . . . and I'd hate both of us for it, but I knew that was the way it was going to be."

Beyond the kitchen door came a low murmur of men's voices and somewhere out in the night a horse whinnied. He looked down and saw that her face was lifted. He put his arms against her, she swayed close, and for a vivid second he saw her lips tremble, then he covered them with his mouth and a great heat swept up over him. The voices beyond the kitchen faded out for a timeless moment, then she threw her arms upward around his neck and pressed into him the full length, and broke clear.

From the doorway Abel cleared his throat before solemnly asking: "Is the coffee ready, Sue? These fellers done a lot of riding."

Abel and Crownover exchanged a long gaze as Sue turned back toward the stove, then Abel made a gentle smile and disappeared beyond the doorway.

"Burt?"

He moved forward, but she maneuvered so that he could not look into her face. "Yes?"

"Will it all end now?"

He was perplexed by the question, not knowing precisely what she meant. "Well, as far as Richmond's concerned, I think it will. He'll go to jail. As for the others . . . I don't rightly know. I suppose most of the riders will go free. About Abel"—he thought of her father's wise ways and easy aplomb; it did not fool him any longer, but he was positive it would fool others—"I don't think you have to worry about Abel."

In a very faint way she said: "I didn't mean . . . that."

He put forth a hand and felt her body turn loose at his touch. "I'd like for you to marry me," he said. "Is that what you meant?"

"Yes."

His hand laid heavy. "Yes . . . what?"

In a tone he scarcely heard, she said: "Yes, Burt. I'll marry you."

GUNS
IN OREGON
LAURAN PAINE

Nobody ever ended up in Younger, Oregon, unless he had specific business there. Which was why Deputy Sheriff Jim Crawford was so suspicious when Edward Given rode into town. Folks had no idea why he was there, but they did know Given had the fastest draw they'd ever seen. And those skills came in mighty handy when a group of well-organized cowboys attacked their town and rode off with all the money in their safe. Now Crawford has no choice but to trust this stranger if he wants to catch the thieves. Yet the unlikely pair soon discovers that the robbery was just a cover for an even bigger operation—and that Given is not the only one in town with secrets.